Thomas Frick was born in Kentucky and has lived in Arkansas, England, Michigan, New York City, Boston, Strasbourg, and Los Angeles, where he is currently a writer, editor, and publishing consultant. Frick has received numerous awards and fellowships for his widely published essays, criticism, and fiction. This is his first novel.

BURNING BOOKS · SANTA FE NEW MEX · MMXI

The Iron Boys

Thomas Frick

For Mitch, who, by instruction and example, taught me how to edit even such things as this. Excelsior!

Tom
1 December 2011
Los Angeles

A QUADRANTS SERIES NOVEL

THE IRON BOYS © 2011 Thomas Frick
THE QUADRANTS SERIES © 2011 Burning Books

All rights reserved. This book may not be reproduced, in whole or in part, for any reason, or by any means now existing or yet to be developed, without consent in writing from the author.

A portion of this book (in an earlier version) was previously published as "From The Iron Boys" in *Agni Online* (November 2006) and as "I Ragazzi di Ferro" in *Buràn* no. 3 (September 2007).

EDITING, DESIGN, AND PRODUCTION: Burning Books

COPYEDITING: Melody Sumner Carnahan, Diane Armitage, Lynn Larsen, Janice Margolis, and Sarah Skenazy

BOOK AND COVER DESIGN: Michael Sumner

ISBN: 978-0-936050-35-5 limited edition paperback

INQUIRIES MAY BE ADDRESSED TO THE PUBLISHER:
Burning Books, P. O. Box 2638, Santa Fe, NM 87504,
www.burningbooks.org; or to the author at misterfrick@gmail.com

DISTRIBUTED BY: Small Press Distribution, www.spdbooks.org

Published and printed in the United States of America.

The Iron Boys and the author
dedicate this book to
Janice Margolis,
its stalwart, constant,
and openhearted champion.

The
Iron Boys

RICKY DID IT

Ricky did it. Ricky did it. Ricky did it. Very first thing that bird say to me that day. Neverll I forget it. Eighteen aught somethin there about. Ever year since come out a that year. Thats the year the birds begin to talk. Why do years got numbers I wonder. Seem like they didn always. Eighteen what off I mark it. April. Im crossin the field up beyond the mullein slope. Where Old Jasper had his sackin shed. Used to be a sheeps keep. Course you wont know that now. All the inclosures. Builders draggin in iron shafts an gear wheels. Boilers spittin out chunk an scut. Engine oil all over. Now ever pile a shithouse brick got a mayor an a magistrate. Well I dont go up there no more. Look at me now. Corbel Penner. Use to be at home on my heels with my name in my mouth. Now Im nothin but a old stump sittin in the shade without these two iron wheels rollin under me arse. Wernt it lovely though to have two roamin legs when the world was young. Course I aint old yet. Not quite. But you know how that goes.

Air smell like fresh cake that day. Not a thought in the world an sudden as your aunts granny a little pipper hop down on a branch right beside this ear. Start flickin his tail an talkin to me. *Ricky did it. Ricky did it.* Well what a that youre thinkin. An Im thinkin it too. So I ask him back. *Whos Ricky. Whadideedo. Whos Ricky. Whadideedo.* An you know that scruffy little fistful he cork over his red an yellow head. Bead me with his eye look just like a apple seed an says to me. Right to me face mind you. *What if he didn. What if he didn. What if he didn.* Well I got no time for scotch banter so I swat that little pecker off his branch an dang he hit the ground dead as dick diddly. Not a scraw more out of him. Not one more word. So I get no answer to my questions that day. I pluck a little wing feather off him to pick out the next piece a apple peel get stuck in my teeth. That little guy he might a been a nutbeater I reckon. Or a beehatch or wax tit what all I know about em. Never did learn the proper names a things. Only Ricky I knowd then was Pank House. Called Ricky by some I dont know why. He didn like it. Next day Im thinkin on what it is Pank done that might start a bird to talkin. Me at that time I aint yet killt a man.

So its a day or two later. Im workin for George Withy as I done back then. Sometimes in the manufactory proper. Sometimes doin this an that for the man hisself. Im sleepin at the sack house. There aint enough light to make you roll over yet. Then I hear him again. Differnt little guy there on the window sill. Cock bunting it could be this time or maybe a screwtail lark. He stretch up his beak. Throat all swole out proud. Chirp as sharp as a pump handle creak. *Ricky did it. Did it did it. Ricky did it. Did it did it.* Then he sit there quiet. Tip his head back an forth lookin down at me. First one side then the other. Thats a rum thing about birds. Got two eyes so they cant decide. Its just the touch a dawn as I say. So I talk to the little guy quiet as I can. Tryin not to wake nobody though you dont want to whisper to a bird. He will not understand you. I figure I charm a little rhyme at him. *Pretty little bird. What say you. Did he or didn he. Tell me do.* Now some a the ladies they think if its a bird its pretty. Simple as that. Tween you an me just like the ladies some is an some aint.

However. It is a fact as the Black Book says. *A cage full a birds is a house full a lies.* Pretty or no a birdll twit you twenty times to tell you one thing true. So when this little guy fly off I think god rid an fare well an I would a gone right back down to sleep. But then the mornin whistle up at Withys put steam in my ears an the mill hammers start clankin again like never before.

Week or so on Pank hisself may a answered my question without my even askin. Ever ones at the Green Lion. Its fightin hour. Mill people all shufflin about. Pay in a pisspot. Poundin on the tables. Panks hunched down in his coat. Im sittin next to him tryin to tell if its water in the bitter or whats wrong with him now. You hear a Ned Ludds army he says. He dont hardly move his lips except they come down on the M when he says army with a kind a snarl. I says Ludds name be on everbodys tongue. You got your petitions Pank says. Your songs. Your letters in the *Notifier*. Its Ned Ludd this. Ned Ludd that. Ned Ludd piss an Ned Ludd shat. Ned Ludds weavin em in Pank says. Theys startin to call him King. Thats the story any road. But whos doin the weavin he says. An whos tellin the story.

Then Pank pull out a little leather pouch. Bout the size you can hide inside your fist if you got to hide it an your fist is big enough. In heres Iron Seed he says. Iron Seed. You ever see that before. What come from plantin Iron Seed I says. Must be Iron Apples. Just a jest but Pank look at me like I know somethin. Shakes the bag. Little shump shump in there. Many a these be sowed all over now he says. Ever sheep meadow garden plot an green yonder. What rise up is your black smoke everwhere bloomin out the factory stacks. What you doin with em then I says. Here he says. He take somethin from his inside pocket. Look like a horseshoe but not much biggern a babys tongue. I says thatd shoe a pony bout the size a my dog. Course I aint had a dog since Rat Tail Jack run off an Pank know that. You watch he says. Pulls out a old king a hearts. Hands me over that horseshoe pointin up. Says hold this like this. Drops some Iron Seed onto the card. Bout as much as two pinch a snuff. Now bring that up under slow he says.

Well I almost fall off a my stool. That Iron Seed jump round like I dont know what. Like them swirly canker knots where they sawed the limbs off a that big old walnut tree used to stand outside the Lion. Black Woppers eyes we use to call em. Pank he tap that seed quick back into the pouch. We drink a while. Ever so often he stare across the table at me like he want me to know what hes thinkin without his sayin it. Swingin that pouch a seed like a clock weight there on the long cord. Wipes the ale foam on his sleeve. Pries the horseshoe out a my fingers. We be the Iron Boys now he says. Ned Ludds men thats a differnt thing. They say they go under ground. We go inside the seed. What we do is magnetize it. Sow it with a spell. Aint no golden age here about. No more silver neither. Thats certain. Iron age an so be it. Our new crops is gonna drive out the old. Well thats the first I hear of it. Wernt a week go by before Pank give me my own pouch a seeds an little horseshoe an a knave a diamonds to go with it. So I can help spread the word about the Iron Seed. Like the Black Book says. *Iron sharpeneth iron. Thus a man sharpeneth the countenance of his friend.*

Few days on Im stoopin for champignons. Up there in the flush shade a the sleepy sisters. Thats what I call em. Them big old trees left all alone when they clear off South Pightle for the coal road. Hardly move your feet an you fill up two big side sacks. I dont know what it be like now. But Im pickin the new pearl whites for the Widow Dedoray over to French Town. Had a darn permanent swell for her daughter Silvy. Go on half a year or so. I bring Widow some *chose choisie* she call it to tease me. Bein come from France. Fine pickins. She dont seem to mind if I stay with Silvy up in the hay shed a day here an a night there. Silvy dont mind neither. Widow she speak our tongue just enough to make me say this an that. Call her Veuve an such like. She an Silvy laugh an talk into each other some times so I dont know what Im thinkin even in my own words.

Never could tell about them two. Widows husband killt somewhere. They come here from the French wars about all I know. Lot a French up French Town way. Lot a comin an goin back then. That night Veuve cook them fairy caps down into a nice slew with new butter. Fried porridge along side. Sweetwater mead to float it all on. Veuve pour me it out slow in a tall French glass. Never saw the color shine like that before. I slop mead in a mug when I get it which is hardly ever. But I mark her dimple smirk an I can picture one or two sharp wags might a brung over that mead. Silvys cheeks is gettin red though shes not hardly drinkin it.

Some reason I feel dumb as a door knob sittin there suckin my lips. Knowin what I come round for with my grimy sack a champignons. Widow she go all slack an sad. Says her own name several times. Dedoray.

Dedoray. Got a mournful thread a French music to it none the less. She run her hand down Silvys hair over an over. I say somethin but it come out all flat there over the table. I cant help bein burnished up inside though. Slip a little smile over to Silvy but she wont look back to me. Not from blushin neither. Somethin other I can tell. Soon it get to be with or without her Id do better bein outside than sittin there lookin into her mamas sad eyes. You can get lost in there cause its a foreign country. I bid em good night an carry my bag back to the shed. Before I go up the ladder I slump down on the barrel half an stretch my legs out for a pipe. Sheen a the meads boilin off my face an Im still a little wobbly tell you the truth.

Bout the time a night you cant tell a cow flop from a countin stone Silvy come out an scurry on by without a nuzzle. Shy with her aint far from sly so I grab at her dress but shes clambered up the ladder ahead a me. I get up there shes layin face down in the sackin I once stuff full a fresh meadow bells. We long since flatten that out sure an dur. Im thinkin it might be time for me to stuff it up new though thats a job a work. First time she was like a little meadow bell. I tell her that. The strong delicate shakin is what I mean. But I didn know what she could understand much a the time. Truth is thats part a what get me all boiled up about her. Ever thing has to be spoke with a touch here an a motion there. Kiss a this an a taste a that. Aint no word for it whether it be whisky or water. Or theys a word you dont know but you both pretend to. Then just us lookin in at each other like who can you be.

But now our nest is all flattened out an Silvys tryin to hide herself in it. I crawl my fingers up under her dress to hope she smile round at me. But she pull up an sit starin at the wall planks. Holds herself tight. Swayin with a little whimper. I didn know what to do or what it all mean. I try an put it together in my mind with Widow lookin at me odd an singin Dedoray her sad French name. But I wernt sure a that neither. Clangy mead is still makin my thoughts runny. So I just press myself up against her. Feel her shiverin little breath bones jerk two three times. I yearn to know what could have her holdin her sobbin inside like that. I scrabble up some straw into a mound an plump up the sackin an button off her dress an lay it over. Im startin you know but she wriggle off with a shiny streak down from each eye. Alls I can do then is turn her real slow. An then it over take us an my face get wet from hers. Im bout to bust big the whole while Im rockin. Tell ya though. Theres a iron achin been come on me for some months down there. Deep inside under it when I get hard like. Was it tryin to tell me somethin I wonder. Might a worried me some but the only times I feel it I aint stop to worry bout nothin.

Teeth is bitin teeth like you do an we buckle up against it. Little ptou ptou she go. Thats the way she use to laugh to drip spit in my mouth. Im right there ready an I know just where she is too. Aint nothin like that knowin an I knowd it with her better than any one. Her fingers clawin on my back. Mine scoopin to lift her. An we Jack an Jill it down that steep hill quick to the bottom where you just lie there dizzy bloomin sweat an tryin to catch your breath. Then Silvys shiverin so we dress her all back up an me too. Sit there shinin an she do look silvery an I tell her so. Dont know why it always surprise me. Shes a water baby an a moon child an all them silver things. She draw her soft hand round my chin. Which feel as sharp on me as old rye stubble. Must a been rough on her silky cheeks.

Dont know why I think of it just then but I pull out my bag a seed an little horseshoe an knave a diamonds an I shows her all of it. A look I never seed before cross her face while beholdin the swirly ring a Iron Seed. Its just Black Woppers eyes I says. Cause Black Wopper make her laugh just me sayin it. But now she say no. Not good not good. She make me pour the Iron Seed back in the bag careful not to spill a tiny bit. Then she run the thong twice around like a ladys packet. Tucks it in my pocket. Presses on it like to say seal it away for another day but never again come what may. Thats what it seem like. Then Silvys holdin herself tight an shiverin again an lookin off like a dark cloud go over. So I lick off her dried up tears an whisper Ill take her back now. Inside if she want. Though I never did go in afterwards before. There at the door I hold her from behind an push my face in that long hair that smell like a sweet breeze blowin round her an me. She stumble her hand back an cup me where my swells gone down. That black throbbin I speak of start to burn like a piece a coal in the steam box. But then she slip through the door quick an dont want me to follow I guess or let the chill in. I didn see her face or say good bye.

Some times the worst pain dont hurt at all right away but only later. I walk far along into the night not feelin my feet. Come out on a knoll I didn know but two trees on guard. Roll up my empty sack behind my head an lose myself up amongst the stars. French silver giggles. Veuve an Silvy talkin behind their hands. Them unknown tongues an whispery things roam all round inside me. Are there birds out there what speak French I wonder. Them stars look near. But all the footsteps on the earth be a vastly number an Im alone in the middle of em an half of em feel like mine right now.

An then. Right in that stretch when your face feel the first light but no airs stirrin that dang bird come back. Dream or waken I darent say. But there it is him again. Him or another. Soft now. Across the meadow where mornin already start to crawl across the ground. That sound cut through the air like a whistle knife. *Ricky did it. Ricky did it. Ricky did it.* I keep my eyes shut an whisper like to someone lyin next to me. Or may be to the stars. If Ricky did it I will too. If Ricky did it I will too. An I swear somebody out there hear me.

The lay a the land be your feet. Get your legs chopped off at the knee like mine it crumple up your map. Cant no longer call the place your own. Even now some times I feel my legs is hangin on me. I want to pull my boots off. Scratch the tickle right up in the arch or on the chub a the heel. Well aint no boots an aint no arch but theys sure still the damn itch be somewhere. An my toes they still burn some times. Like what you hear a them confessions. When they stick your feet in the flames after rubbin em thick with mutton fat. You get tired a that fast an tell em what ever they want. Be good to feel them hard rungs under foot again though. Countin em all the way. Four five an six an lookin up at Silvy.

But when your legs go through the iron gate before the rest a you. Well then I say its fair to ask em. Can they give me a sign from over there. Just to tell me whats ahead. They owe it to me. Cause they know an I dont. Itchin an burnin make you think theys sunk part way down in hell fire. An you want to know if thats whats gonna come. Though I aint done so much thats bad I reckon. Any ways its my head should be whats punished. Not my legs. Most times they just go where I tell em to. Even when they shouldn. Some days I roll myself over to the ice house an push my stumps against them cold blocks in that nice dim room by the river. They like that. They aint so restless.

Used to spend my time roamin all around these portions. I knowd all your roads an rangers. I been called wanderer an worse. Wanderer sure. Though I aint nern to scuttle off like a wing bug if some man call a fool a knave an there be fightin over it. No matter where you go there be *on the one side the glowing mire. An on the other the ditchy quag.* Thats from the Black Book I reckon or some other ilky pilgrim fodder. *Turn not left or right. Remove thy foot from evil. Ponder the path an let all thy ways be set out like flag stones in the sun. Let your eyes look steady on an keep your eye lids straight before you. Put back a froward mouth an perverse lips put far from thee.* Well I try an do all that though its hard to keep it in your mind. You can ask me about perverse lips but what is a froward mouth. Any way the roads always alive an gloatin. The trail knows where Im goin. Many times Id light in a place for a fortnight. Even longer. Legs try to tell me no sir. Dont stay here. They kick me over in the dark. Want back on the road I guess. I almost wonder if they knowd what were gonna happen to em. Once I hole up in Golspie go on ninemonth. Dont remember why. But I tell you. Even if you got your legs your map now days is gone as good. Even your wandrin minstrels aint bringin new songs no more.

You seen them big foldout sheet maps down at the court house. All the trees an hills is drawed in though kind a stubbly. All the buildins too what was builded at that time or scribbled in later. I seen one page for this half shire it got most everthing. Got the false fork in the Runny Pumps road. Got the dry pond. Got the flags on the poles. Must be theys the ones left over from the summer when them harlequins set up a tent show on the road to Raw Morton. Though the way them flags is pointin there on the map the wind that day it must a blowed in ever direction at once. Well some times it do that sure an dur. But that map what it dont got of all things is George Withys manufactory. Dont got anything built since then neither. Court house maps the last map made a these parts I believe. Changes come faster than you can make a map now days.

Well that feisty peeper what I slap down I must a felt bad about him. Next few weeks I swear them birds start hoppin an flingin themselves round me like the eyes a Dolly Eager. So I do some calculatin an cogitatin an though it aint exactly as the Black Book says you got to bless the birds. Bless em in spite a their contrary nature. For they may be the fluffy flyin eye balls a god. Think on it. Just about the right number of em. See out a both sides at once. Go anywhere. Many differnt sizes. Coats a many colors. All this *Ricky did it. Ricky did it. Ricky did it* an such may be to distract me from what it is them birds is actually doin or watchin out for. That in mind I decide to keep my own eyes open. Listen for French birds too on account a Silvy an the Widow.

Ned Ludds army now this is another bit to puzzle on. First Ned Ludd I hear of is a idiot lad smash up a stockin frame down in Bell Misty long ago or some say in Peterlawn. This Neds nothin but a drooly mumbler an your roisty boys is tauntin him as they will. What I hear is he flare up an smash ever thing around him without thinkin much. Not one to lead a army as any one can see. If yous lookin for a idiot to lead you our own New Billy fit that description. An some do try to make it out that New Billy is Ned. Which justify Panks wariness about this so called King Ludd an his men. Whos doin the weavin. An whos tellin the story. Thats what Pank say we got to keep in mind.

Our New Billy he do bad things but you cant blame him for it. You just got to chase away what creep in behind his eyes from time to time an turn em hard like wet flint. Like New Billy carry around a stone mug which be his cup an his toy an his basher. You cant pry it from his fingers even to fill it with hot soup. Some times he dip it in the bucket an dash water on his head when he get food up his nose or crawl into nettles. But he wont wash his self even like a animal. Cant or dont. He end up stampin an cryin an flailin. Or he use that mug to beg with. Dont need to. He just see some a them alms folk I expect an imitate their surly motions. Folk give New Billy any thing they want to. Rose Stonewarden once water down some porter for him but that wernt a good notion. Billy beg mice from old John Piper who give him some from time to time. Mice is six a penny comin an goin. John Piper get that much from George Withy to rid em from the factory. An that much again from Timothy Twist who feed em to his snakes. Twist also buy mice for the Mechanick Arts Society. Desmond Carke was deliverin hay there once an seen em put a mouse to sleep under a glass bell an wake it up again by pointin fingers at it six times in two minutes. He wont go there no more. Too much witchery he says.

I seed New Billy cram a mouse down in his mug an mash it with a ladle. Laughin an his eyes hard an sparkly like someone else behind them eyes know what they doin. But Billy dont know. I say child but how old is he. No one know. I guess he be called New Billy cause ever time its like he never know nothin before. It all be all new to him. Thats what Rose Stonewarden say anyway an she knowd him best. Same old Billy to us though. Eyes a goggle. Fat curly lip drippin what ever he last suck on or chew. Could be anything still hangin there or drippin. Billy some ways remind me a Rat Tail Jack. Droopy tongue dog who attach his self to me long back. Jackll shirk about his guttery business here to Colmehin Dale an back an never oncell look at you. Dont much notice him for days then all a tremble hes pawin your knee an catchin your gaze an he peer right into you.

Like some kind a pleadin leap out a his wet eyes. As though hes askin you for the last bit he need to stand up an talk. But then next thing he look aside an forget all about it. Off sniffin whatever rank business like a usual dog. You just want to kick him for pretendin or for not tryin hard enough. All you got in the end is a ugly dog with unnatural thoughts. I swear he give me a chill that old mange arse wobbler. But I was sorry when he run off from me like he never think a me no more. Long time ago now. You never know whats in a dogs mind. New Billy somewhat like that. Folk use to tease him. Tell him all about some outland fling an he dont know nothin. Smile along. Maggie Moats use to sing to him to get him to leave off his bad doins. It get to be a song round here. I even seen it printed down in a book. He run to Maggies window an let out some yobbin wail he must think be singin. Maggie pull off a hank a her soft sugar bread for him an go like this.

O New Billy my charm a New Billy
When shall I see my New Billy again
When the fishes fly over the fountain
Then I shall see my New Billy again
When your fishes fly over the fountain
Then you shall see your New Billy again.

Dont much like that sugar bread myself. No good for arse wipin. Leave you with a sticky bum. Maggie can never tell if New Billy knowd he be the one she singin about. She use to say Billy dont you remember. When that big flat flounder fly right over that fountain. How you clap your hands an try an catch it. New Billy turn red laughin even though he dont know what shes talkin about. An we bustin bubbles laughin at him he look so odd. He dont know what teasin is.

I spect it was my Great Mam first tell me bout Ned Ludd. Not by name. But she talk about the fog a the machines. All that was gonna happen. I remember one time not long fore she go up. I wernt mindin my elders much those days. Must be Ise all a fourteen annos nigh on twenty one. Fartin live coals ever direction. I didn at all like lookin at Great Mam. She was most a hunnerd then. Spotty narrow flabs swingin off her arm bones thin as two whistle sticks. Gone bald on top in witchy patches. Eyes runnin cloudy yellow. Somethin red an white pooch out the bottom a one of em. I never want to look too close. Blind folk you know theys always thinkin you doin somethin you aint.

She grab my hand. Look to me Carby she says. Its Corbel I says. Corbel Penner I tells her but she only hear what she want. I dant see you so much Carby but I know who you be. Dont you forget now. You got your fathers name she says. Well I dont know nothin a my father so this be nothin I need hear about. Look to my eye Carby. Cloudy moon. See right there she says. Cloudy moon right there come from black fog come over this land. Look to my eye Carby. I show you that fog. Come here. Come on up. Come up she says. Hold my hand a spell. Well I didn even move but she pinch my knuckles tight as tinsnips. Look she says. Look a me eye here. You can see it right here. She pulse my hand tighter an start to rub on my wrist hard with them crooked fingers. Cloud or fog she says. Cloud or black fog when machines come on the land. No one see it. No one see. But I see it. An you can see it in me. White cloud. Cupidy sheep. Sing me to sleep. Black fog. Hear the *mooo* in the murk. Hear the *baaa* in the black iron dark. Huddly cow woe not cross no iron road. I may be old Carby she says. Old is old. But Big John Brown aint gonna shit the devil from his gut after he swallow him down kickin with salt bread an butter. An I never yet see a tin soldier brew good hop beer in a broken egg shell.

She go on like that a while. I scorn it then not knowin what shes on about. Then some big thing brighten up her face. May be a cloud move off behind me. *Yessssss* she hiss. Suckin in air. I know you Carby. All them folk workin for machines they weave that black fog over the land. They dont see it but it cover ever thing. Then shes spittin in my palm. Breathin on it an rubbin it with them gnarly bone fingers I try to pull away from. Its like she want to read the future in there. Listen to me Carby she says. I dint teach you letterin for you to sign your name X an think that come before C. You got a big thing to do. Char the iron. Plant the seed. Swear the oath. Forge the deed. Well she got a lot a dumb doves flappin in her rafters so I dont think much of it then. I pull away an dont look back. Star a my hand ache for three days after from her pinchin it. But it strike me now. Her talkin about the oath an the seed. The iron an the deed. Time circle round an you cant tell what come before what. Whad she really know back then an howd she know it.

You dont know what be the cause a what. For instance Nancy. Shes the first one I could say the word love about an mean somethin. One day long ago Im straddlin a big old dead tree got laid across Whisker Floss for a foot bridge. Wernt too far from Child Town. Used to go there where I could tell myself what to do an how to do it. Low dark cloud hang a fat chill on the air that day. Water black an windin fast around the bend. Three four Child Town lads is playin stick an benjamin like I aint there which is fine by me. Im launchin bark boats an each one take me to a differnt far away place. Except the ones that get hung up but they dont count.

Barefoot Nancy an her pretty skirts she hop back an forth behind me on the damp bank singin a little game she want me to note but pretendin not to see me.

> *I love a tree more than a man*
> *I love a bird more than a tree*
> *I love a cloud more than a bird*
> *I love the moon more than a cloud*
> *I love a star more than the moon*

I sling a wet stick back at her over my shoulder. I can feel her not lookin at me right down in my belly. She go on but slower. Then you say *I love the sun more than a star*. Then I say *I love the dawn more than the sun*. Come dance with me Corbel wont you she says. You have the next one. Next one what I says. Come here she says. It takes two to do it proper. Them Child Town boys is nowhere about now. We has to move up the bank to the bleachin flat to find enough room.

> *Arch hand over turn through under*
> *Each on each then step back four*
> *Arch hand over turn through under*
> *Each on each then step back four*
> *First to north*
> *Then to west*
> *Then to south*
> *Then to east*
> *Arch hand over turn through under*
> *Each on each then step back four*

Then she says *I love the dawn more than the sun*. An I says *I love the mist more than the dawn*. An she says *I love a man more than the mist*. An I says *I love a tree more than a man*. An you see Im startin back at the beginnin. Im sayin her lines an shes sayin mine. Never did figure why that work like that. But when she says *I love a bird more than a tree* an when I says *I love a bird more than a tree* it mean two differnt things. To the bird especially.

Roll me over by the wall there would you. Feel like I got rats gnawin on my sittin bones. Just one more thing for a man to endure. Sun use to shine right here all through the afternoon. No wall there then. So be it. I like the shade more anyways now. You see that purple blossom back ayond there in the slanty patch a sun light. Too bright for my eyes over there. I forget what that be called. Toadwinkle. Rattle jenny. Somethin like that. This green red thing here drop down a string a hearts under ever leaf. Thats called pink mary. An over there. The ones with the long leafs what look like fingers. That they use to call chase a cripple. Desmond Carke he use to hide a bunch in his pocket an fling it at me. As if them names mean any thing.

You see that there fat brown wiggly creeper all over the place. Thats thwacks. Never growd round here till Withys manufactory come in. Now you cant stop it. Grabber shoots choke off ever fresh stalk they can find. Just like men. Pullin each other down instead a helpin each other up. You even find thwacks down in the pond. Everwhere. I hear folk say its good for runnin mumps or golden carbuncles or somethin. That lady from Twine Hill come by now an again she sell you a compress or infusion she call thwacks be nimble. I had carbuncles once. Wernt golden but still worrisome. I aint took such medicine an I get to be just fine without. If you think Im fine. What I think is some folk just go all crazy brained on you an you cant do nothin about that. Like when they say they got them mill bugs nippin in they unders. Well I spent my time in the factory an I never seen them mill bugs nor suffered from em neither. Im incline to doubt em altogether. Ask me its a pure case a riddle rash. Aint no compress or infusion a thwacks is gonna cure that.

Thwacks though. Here to stay look like. *If I should prosper in such vegetal profusion* like they say. After Silvy leave I used to think what will become a me. Will I end up with a old oak wife who wont mend the seat a my trousers fore she be marchin me around with her loads a laundry or what not in a womans basket. Them was some bad mornins after Silvy leave. *I saw deaf death in the old mans eye. But deaf death could not hear me cry.*

Well. My mind keep turnin corners. I cant stop it. But you dont want to forget nothin. Even if it be all twisted up an in the wrong order. If thats the way it come back to me then there must be somethin right about it. So that Nancy. Cant get her out a my mind all a these years. But I cant get her well enough into it neither. How she once look I couldn chalk it for you now. Its so long ago. Couldn draw you what it were about her even could I draw. Try to cull her up nothin come but a little pink smudge an some winsome curly patches in the dark behind my eye lids. You ask me blue eyes or brown I cant even say an aint that a sad thing. You dont see the water. You see the stone in the pool or your knee in the bath. I remember this. Her little cheek corners they hold back a smile that dont ever quite get to be a smile under her wide eyes that look blowed up like shes whistlin. Them eyes close slow an her kiss be a soft frown she press hard on you. Always a frownin kiss though she didn scorn to press it.

Nance she got a head swirlin full a long thick chestnut hair. Rich an plump an look like she should be laughin as she toss it back though she never laugh. Nancys mama brush it with good long boar bristle in a ivory handle. Every day Nancy sit there in the door yard. Missy Primskirts frownin on her little dolly chair. Two hundred strokes her mama count. Be glad Corby Nancy says. She call me that an I dont care. Glad a what I says. Glad there arent two hundred steps to our dance. Her eyes is closed an there aint nothin on her face. Or there be somethin but I dont know what it is. Some days I come by try an make her squirm by makin faces. It dont work. Her mama watch me sideways. Says look here Corbel. She hold up a hank. Shiny as Nancys cherry wood dowry chest she says. Which gets French polish every day. An Nancys hair gets nothing but goose oil mixed with Spanish lavender an sweet belly rue.

Then come the sad day. It was after I had spit some apple seeds an juice an chunks one day all down the front a Nancys fresh white smock an she run off home red faced. When I get there later mamas countin with her lips as she pull the brush. Nancys still poutin though in a fresh white blouse. Cept for mamas white hair an a few care lines about the eyes she look so much like Nancy I dont like it. You dont want to think a your girl lookin like her mama so soon. Her father he was scarred bad an blinded by a horse whip long ago. He sit there with the two of em in good weather. Smilin off out in the day somewhere.

It must a been the evenin sun poke from behind a cloud just when Nancy shake her head. Her hair boil up in a red mist you can see through. Then her mama jerk it rough behind her ears for the second hundred an I see Nancys head back lit like she got no hair. It look so awful small. No moren a demi cannon ball. Look just about the size a what I glimpse once a her downy melons. That was when I lie behind her house one night. Try to catch a sight a her shy places. Or her mamas. It dont matter. But ladies devilish blockades is laid up against you when you be groanin for such sweet revelation. A closin door cut off the fall a Nancys gown when she drop it on the floor to dress for bed. Slant of a mirror wont quite let me feed my eyes on mamas bust as she wind it up in gauze by candle light. Exact drape a their clothin cut my eyes off at each legly bend an turn. Ladies is most expert in the swings an sways a fabric as they move. My eyes get sore from over stretchin. So I close my lids an next thing I know Im stumblin up stiff an sleep cheeked in the dawn to get away before Im caught for a low peep grubber by missus out to pick the mornin eggs. Im scuffin up the tracks Ive wore under the windows when right there six inches from my face is Nancys corpy peaches an each little strawberry tip near to pressin on the glass pane as she wrestle her night dress up over her head. Them debbies is rounder an much biggern youd think the way she keep em tuck down under the starch a her blouses. Though they flatten out some with her arms raised high in holy surrender to my inflammation.

But now her mamas pullin her hair back an Nancys heads a swayin bulge like them bare melons in the window. But out a place. With her neck stretched back her nose is just a pudge blob with two big holes in it. Nothin like that sweet strawberry kiss in the middle. Nancys fine nose use to be the anchor of her brow an the pointer of her regal gaze. Once upon a time it hook me like a fish even when she wernt lookin at me. An now her ears is stickin out a this bulb like curlin flaps with coils inside too wiggly to laugh at. An I never had to think a Nancy with a chin before. Cause its her lips an the curvin of her mouth you look at tween them cheeks. But now her chin stick out like a bad rock in a road. Her whole body droop like a poor animal. Like a sheared sheep or when you see a long hair dog come out a the pond. Her mamas still intent on brushin like nothins changed. But Im seein Nancys face like itll be years on. Just where the fleshll droop an how her eyes will turn down sad because a whatll happen in her life. I dont want to see all this but the picture done been tacked into the frame.

I couldn stand no more a that terrible soft brushin sound. Soft but there was devils sighin in it. What just one day before was a perfumed curtain hangin round her sweet face. Now its all false fringe. It aint a part a her. Just somethin you rub oil in like a table. My guts is ripped. Whats more her smilin father he cant never see her hair or face or nothin of her. An there I am cant stand to look at her no more. I kick off as slows I can not knowin where to go. An Nancy I can tell she knowd all of it right then. Shes quick callin Corbel with a heart snaggin tiny plaint though with her face to the sky she cant see me go. Just the sight a her like that change both of us. Happen like a cut. We didn cross paths to linger side by side no more. You sidle by each other on the wrong half a the road. You stay away from places. Somethin freeze up in her. She leave off schoolin. Pull away from friends. Grow old. Not right then to look at like a fairy spell but none the less. Never marries what I later hear.

Was it me bein some years oldern her what poison it some how I wonder. Did she want more a me cause a what her mama want. Or was it what I seen that day. Could she a seen what I seed. Even with her eyes shut. Her tale could be writ down like a tragedy I reckon. Strange thing though. I happen to see her a few years on. We pass by each other but she dont look over at me. Dont even know Im there I think. In some other place entire. But I mark what she become is thin an shrouded not round an sad nor bare like what I seen in that vasty moment long ago.

Though from the other view it could be Im the one get caught an drug off to a differnt place. Im the one who see the drainin pond in faces. Nothin fresh no more about the fresh lips of a smile. You see how hinged they is upon the substance a the jaw. Ill say this thing though. Hair it must grow inside your head as well as outside. It got its meanin there no matter how a lady keep her tresses. No matter how close you breathe an finger em. Dont dig beneath that soft illusion. That holy perfume. That be the trap an blessin she prepare for you. It must be hair that keep a womans time in place an bloomin properly. Other wise you see what happen underneath it all. An you dont want to know. Even that first day. Her dance at Whisker Floss. I knowd her pride a hair would come between us. It were the way she hold her face out from her neck so careful like. Only once do her face come back to me. One night I leave the Green Lion an set out runnin cause who want to be anywheres. Run till my sides ache. Fling myself down in the weeds. My eyes is closed an Im tastin dirt an the bloods boomin in my temple. Then clear as a plovers egg in a gold bowl theres Nancys face throbbin behind my eyes. Sharp as that paintin what hang up in Framemakers Inn.

Then my blood run down an my breath drop an I cant see her no more. Ever thing fade out. Ever thing fade when not bloomed up by kisses. An what are all the things we dont remember. Where do they go. Must go somewhere since they once be here. Cant go nowhere. Cause where is nowhere.

> *Tears of iron and sighs of lead*
> *Roll out of my aching head*

Thats what they call doggerel. Thats from William Dogg the poet who come up from Big Town once an stay a brief while. I recall him moanin to the moon when hes lyin there not lookin at the sky cause hes drunk on the floor a Sarah Maldons parlor. I dont got tears a iron but I do got sighs a lead an when theys out a me I get up an brush off an walk back to the Lion cause if you gots to be somewhere where else is there to go.

Apples they was the first good thing turn bad. First thing I knowd of anyway. Happen with Izaac Friars cordon trees a Wicks pippins. Goldenest fruit you ever saw. Prize in Izaacs eyes. He clip an tie an sing his seedlins into that full arch over the path at Six Pins. Right there at the turn a the rise. Ever time you walk under them trees is like you was at some ones weddin. Then one year them pippins come out showin the black spot. Like a penny canker on most ever one of em right up on the cheek. Not soft brown like a bruise. Shiny coal black. Wernt no worms neither. Not in Izaac Friars. You try to cut it out the apple fall apart on you. Black spot must a come from bad seed somewhere down the line. Them apples taste bad too. Rose Stonewarden she say its like a piece a bad metal in your mouth. That bitter shudder. You might ask what does a lady like Rose know about bad metal in her mouth. I cut a apple in half crosswise to show New Billy the star inside an I swear I fling that ding thing away quick. Middles clean gone. No star no seed nothin. Just a round hole with brown mush around the sides. Now that aint right. Them pippins they get fat fast that year an drop untimely. What to do but press em for cider. Izaac Friar he let a man who come through with a empty cart haul all his apples away. Dont give me nothin for em Izaac says. Thats how bad he was on the thing.

Couple months later one cold night that same man come back to Izaacs door. Says I want to give you these twelve jugs to pay for them apples. Would you take em from me sir he says. Izaac says thank you I dont want none a that cider. Man ask hisself in to get warm. Sets down an starts tellin Izaac about the word inside the word. Like a seed inside a apple grow into another tree an put out more apples. Though we may not be here to eat em by an by he says. Izaac tell him you dont use seed but seedlins but it dont stop the man. You look down inside that seed the other way he says. You say a apple be in there. Angels in the world they dont hear apple. They hear somethin else he says. The word inside the word. The seed inside the apple. Mans got a tattered little book he pull out a his pocket. No covers. Missin pages front an back. He rip out two three leaves an hand em to Izaac who give em to me later. Says I dont want em Corbel but you might make out somethin in em. Dont tell me if you do he says. Well I never did an I dont know what happen to em. All kind a crazy language. Izaac ask the man what about my pippins. What about the black spot. What about that brown mush inside. No seed in em. Whyd I want your cider. Well the man says angels an devils they may be fightin to put a differnt seed inside them apples. You may want to pay that some mind. Izaac stand up an thank him for the pages an escort him back out into the cold. Sure enough despite what Izaac say to him theys twelve jugs a cider sittin next to the steps next morn. Izaac put em down cellar to forget it. Couldn bring hisself to thow em out I guess. He may still got em. They did come from his pride a apples. He might a wondered what they turn into. Would a like to ask that fellow what about the word inside the bird. Birds may not know what they mean. But what is it the angels hear.

Hard it is to say what this apple business have to do with George Withy. He be the one who build the manufactory here. George Cogent Meadows Richard Pilfer Withy the Third. Such a string a names is generally bescribed upon you if yous sprouted from a regal tree with wide spreadin relations all around. I wont say spreadin like thwacks. But too unruly to be like Izaacs apples. I guess if you was named like him you would be like him. You look at him even now you see a growd up red cheek baby with a golden chain a numbers round his neck. Grandfather in India. Lieutenant Governor Pilfer Withy. Three feathered hats an six places to put em. Sterile bandages. Fine slings. Withys medical cloth. If you aint hear of it he will tell you till you swear you do have. First used in the royal surgeons college. Export to Holland Denmark Spain Withy says. Written up in the *History of Trades and Manufactures.*

An then his father. George Cogent Meadows Richard Pilfer Withy the Second. Mattin. Battin. Bobbin threads. Wicks an rope. Withy Bombay hemp. Tarpaulins. Sail cloth an coal sacks. You might call it nothin but roughery. But then they corner the world wide trade in imperial sashes. Dealin in silks an rare dye stuffs. George Senior invent the phrase *Something For Every One.* You must a heard that fish face lie. Then the new so called slogan. *One Size Fits All.* Which would be a lie even if it was true. Which it aint.

Our George Withy he rise up through the firm. Fine fabric on machines the thing for him. Them new inventions allow him specialities he never have the skill for. Cathedral lace. Petty coats. French cuffs. Curtain edges. Please the finer ladies Strassburg to Philadelphia. Im just tellin you what he tell you. He dont got fingers enough to tick off all he need to count. You hear the story of his factory nine a dozen times. But then come the troubles. Napoleon. Channel blockades. Withy take it as a personal attack. Not the way to run a proper business he says. Hes always rubbin his chin like hes polishin a scryin stone. Starin into the beyond. You find him that way more oft than not. Three assembly men was sent up from Big Town. Lookin into the weavers complaints. Vestigatin your factory smashins which has started here an there. Not much a that come yet to our half shire so this be a safe place to cast their eyes about. Withy he jump right up top a box an start declaimin. Im up a ladder that day polishin the windows of his office what look out over the factory floor so Im hearin all the puffage of his bluster.

Big idea he says. Its biggern a country. Now how can you tell me thats a bad thing he says. Every thing taken up by the hand a man is a machine. For what is a machine but what make that very hand a man stronger than his fingers be without it. Some benighted folk in Southing this very month gone by they have destroyed sixteen lace machines he says. What is their purpose. Why not destroy the plough. What is a plough but a good ploughin machine. Ever man he want a plough an a wife an which one first is your good guess. Maybe even plough the wife ha ha. What then. Shall I till broad acreage with a spade he says. Or with my bare an crafty hand if crafts your cry. Your spade. Your scythe an flail he says. Them too be machines. But go. Go I tell you. *Rub forth the corn with thine own hand and winnow it in thy breath* if you wish to pledge your loyalty to the purest ways a man. I dont preach against the Black Book he says. But without machines you have no water wheel. No hand cranked mill. No treadle for the lolling feet. These too be machines he says. You never think a that I wager. Now Withy be puffed up like a fat crow on a fence post. An when someone like him keep sayin a word like *machine* it be smooth. *Machine* like French cloth. *Machine* it start to even be a comfort in your ear.

Come let us blister our palms together gentlemen he says. I welcome you. With Robinson Crusoes pestle we shall grind our alien corn. But then verily I say unto you only one in a thousand shall have aught to sup upon. The rest shall starve. So be it if thats your dish. Not that we eat more now but there be ever more that eat he says. Although you ask me I think Withy do eat more to judge from what his tailor let out. My friends he says. We must thank the mathematick gods the only number that will climb faster than peoples propagation is the uncountable rotations of our good machines. He pause an look about an clearly see hisself as more than equal to them Big Town gents. Not just this valley but the world he says. An that be in truth what Withy see. He dont see whats here. He see elsewhere. He see here as part a there. One two three ten. That be Withy. Aint nothin but he triple underline it. Cant make ten into a hundred what good is it. Not This Valley But The World. He mights well carve them words into the sign board on the road to town. Then them Big Town travelersll know they aint arrivin here but everwhere.

The world he says. You know what that means. No end a jobs he tell them Big Town men. One is writin notes an not lookin. The other two theys just suckin up his pap with fat smilin eyes they dont even see out a the tops of. Some folk here Withy says they know what it is Im speakin of. They welcome my investment in vestment if you take my point. Some a the others an maybe not the best they dont like to learn a new thing he says. Wont give up the old ways farthing or fangle. I tell em go do what you want. But you see what happen to em. Some just need encouragement he says. I give em that. Apple or the boot. Take your pick. You can not be lazy no more in this world he says. A man followin the old ways may do a hunnerd differnt things to fill a day. Stitch a work. Then he smoke his pipe. Then he take a walk to spank the ladies. Lullaby the afternoon. Eat drink an relieve his self. Lift up his tail an blow smoke from his arse. Old Sheppey here he read while he weave. Withy wave his hands from side to side. No more a that he says. Readins for Sunday.

Got your machine a man can do one thing all day like a hunnerd men before he says. Another man or woman do another. Your child can do another an it all fit together in gods gearlike wisdom. Like the main shaft up there turn them forty wheels. An straps come down across the floor to power each machine. Just like the Black Book says. *And their work has there a wheel in the middle of a wheel. When the wheels are lifted up the living creatures are lifted up from the earth.* And we are lifted up he says. I am a friend of the Black Book. I start big with eighty men. Now I got eight hunnerd. An that eight hunnerd with machines be like eight thousand a the former sort. Aint no use your frittery home spun labor next to these fine machine spit rows. Tend a machine you play it like a piano forte he says. Take one good lesson an your machine has got the sweeter broader sound if you know how to listen. The coins of commerce gentlemen. They clink in unceasing tumble like a jingling water fall. Just one little thing. Jack an Jill must be nimble here he says. No dozin or you be death slapped when a strap break. Or nippered by the spinnin cogs. Blotched with burns from the coal box. Theres a thousand needles pinkin. You can pierce your fingers an frizz the lace. Got to watch a hawk blink there in the frames he says. But thats the marvel gentlemen. Machines improve men.

Then he invite them assembly men to see all the slappin leather pulley belts a his bleatin pride. Come in come in he says. Like a fat spider to three brother spiders. First showin off his new steam power shuttle web. Ten thousand threads at once he says pointin up to the long drive shaft squeakin end to end between the fanlights. Before your horse empty a feed bag he says I got ten yards a what I call cathedral ratchet lace you can hold up inch to inch against Countess a Pembroke point de venise. You cannot tell a difference. Look a that he says puppetin his hand size samples eye to eye. Look a that. Well them doodad circles an twirlin twists is fine at a glance no doubt. But aint no point de venise. Withy aint afraid a contradiction. No one is truly lookin. You take that piece for your young Sally sir he says. Your daughter a course is who I mean ha ha.

It still amaze me how Withy propel his ruse across the general perception. Any one can tell a difference. No one seem to want to. Them assembly men they finger an nod. Finger an nod. Standin right before the tickin ratchets spillin out the kings own yardage day an night. An no one say a word. What was them gents seein I wonder. Was they seein lace or seein fancy motions a machines. Lookin backwards at it I know that Withy was puffed somewhat from desperation. Orders from the council had cut off French trade. Warehouse in Bastford couldn close its doors from bein over stuffed. Goods is pilin up in the manufactory hallways till you mights well wipe your greasy fingers on the bolts a fine silkeen as you turn sideways to squeeze past em. Decent men be thown off the lines an out the door an some a those

Im speakin of lie back in wait to vent their ire.

Like Sheppey who like to read while he work. He wont brook bein made example of. So here he come wandern out from behind the two tier stockin frame. Seem first like hes a retainer sent to greet the visitors in his old cloth hat. Instead you hear a high vibratin voice you dont know what its sayin at first. Cog a penny. Cog a penny he says. Tampin out his words with a neptune pike on the stone floor. Catch ever ones eye with that thing. Holdin his Black Book in the other hand. Whos he an where he come from theys all thinkin. Cog a penny feed a machine he says. Look at em. All them mill masters want of ye now. Lace chump out like cheap French bunting. Wont stop till youre like to dress the god sake nation in a shroud. Then who be smart he says. Nary stop to see if a new thing be good as a old thing. Nary stop to heed who be needin all this yardage. When they packy boat sit full an no room at the warehouse. They shut us out he says. Hat for a sack. Look a that cog he says. Look a that rod. Sheppey hes got the gents attention pointin with his pike. Ladies sittin at the frames behind dont raise their heads. Theys all dressed up in lace edge finery that day. They was brought in an told look ye pretty an pretend to work. Withys wife Jane she dress em fine for the visitors is what I hear. Them there cog says Sheppey. That may be your son an daughter. Who want they son an daughter be a cog in a machine.

But Withy hes a man who know the moment. Thats what his numbers be the sum of. He pipe up without a slink or hitch. Depend on what machine he says. Ever one laugh an look about an chuff the ruffle in the air like a bunch a diddly birds. Old Sheppey he just dodder out the door an down the high road with his pike pointin the way under the bright late mornin sun an dazzled or damned I guess one a the two he stumble off the road into the new mill pond an float till his head get cut off by the curvin metal wheel blades they install that spring the same time as Withys big new clock. I didn know him much but it seem sad to me that no one mark his passin. Not a word in the *Notifier*. Like they want to forget.

They dint find Sheppey till the next day. Mean time Withy go on like there wernt no interruption. I got myself nary a notion a these works he says. Thats the secret beauty a machinery. Machine know everything it need to know. Worker now just need to know the motions. Man woman an child can tend machines knowin naught a how they work. In that you all be just like me he says. Well this be Withys silken lie. One a the few he outright tell. He help design his machines an have the patents on em. He know them operations very well indeed. We dont be just like him. George Withy though he aint the evilest about. Hard for me to say it but its true. An he depend on us all knowin it. Troubles sure are on the land he says but they cant last. Magistrates here abouts they take too much in lawly liberties. Try to break the frame breakers. Not yet in this town but near enough. I tell em no need for it. Workers fall in line. When they see theys starvin an the others eatin. Plenty folk he says they like to work machines. Talk to old Jarley here. His hands dont hurt no more from them eight pound croppin shears he wield like a tinsmith. But sheriffs men he says. I swear they take a lewd pleasure in all this bangin shootin hangin. An what gods sense in transport now I ask you. I myself he says. Withy say that often. I myself. Who else would he be. I myself he says I save one poor wretch thats bound for kangaroo land. John Gwilt over there. I know him to be a upright fellow an I knowd his father too. I tell em I can use that one. Bucket a ale turn this sheriff south on that one. John dont like me to tell of it Withy says. He hath his loyalties to keep an all so lets move on.

You gentlemen aint like my continental customers he says. I give you monster prices. Today only. All them Dutch vendees an middle men want first an most to see my works. Bring their special fine ground spyin spectacles and surreptitious note books. Frenchmen is generally more content to feel the lace. The Withy name be good as dragons gold. I show you gentlemen far more than I show them he says. For in the guise of custom theys stealin my advances. But here we are. Heres what I can show you. Through this door. On my trust in your graces reticence an the favor of your custom.

By this time Im back down on the floor an followin the group. Dont know what duty Withy think Im doin. May be he judge me a witness to his efforts. Or dont want to break his stride. Most like he dont see me there at all. Only see his numbers an the prospect of increasin em. Big steam engine at the far end he says. Out that door the coal house an the boilers. Above you see the belts up to the drive shaft an loops down to the differnt jobs. Here we have the cardin an the spinnin. Weavin over here. An croppin there. See the circle mounted blades. Cuttin an sewin over there. Lace is under my personal supervision. Thats why I have the windows in my office. Many of you Big Town folk has told me youre adopting my observational designs. Heres finishing an heres packing. Repair shop over there. Engine smithy. Wool room. Countin desk. On an on George Withy go. Where he stop nobody know. He never tire of it. In fact delighted like a boy. Be like New Billy with the ever newness of his smile. Im glad I hear him speechify that day. First time I think about the factory *system* as they call it. Dont know if it help. Somehow it make the factory seem larger and smaller at the same time. An I reckon it do help though I dont know how.

I might tell you Ise ripped off a ear or two in my time an worse but I never cut a man down with the stroke of a pen. But there I am at Fool Fair. First big contest is your jingling match for the flitch a bacon. Old Barley win that one. Desmond Carke win the leg a mutton for pole climbin. I come third past the manger in the cheese race. Ben Maldon he get the buckskin breeches for back swords. Its always them who dont need em get em. There was jumpin in sacks. Ridin the whistle. I sure love to watch the ladies doin that. Beer in a flood. You can imagine. Lalloway win the court house visit for grinnin through horse collars. No surprise there. Then theres the pig line race. I never seed that one before or since. Everbodys bettin on some piglet. They all seem to pretend its the thing to do. To do what I cant figure. It were moren what it look like thats certain. They feed this little black an white porker on beetroot mash an what turn out to be gear oil. They tie its curly tail to a string sixty six feet long an slap it on the rump an watch it go. An when it stop an shit they stake the spot an spin him round an do it again. Well someone must a win somethin. But as if by chance they get them cords strung up right where it turn out the walls a Withys manufactory get built.

Not long after the fairs packed up a little hut appear in the middle a that field. Right at the corner a that first pig line angle. Look like it was sewed together out a old cheese rind. Flimsy stinkin stuff. It sit there an nothin happen three four weeks. One night Im comin round the Knob late from a weeks job in Bastford. Pallorous big moon hangin over Tit Peak. No mist is risin but its like they was a veil pulled over the land. That moon was big I tell you but you couldn even make out the rabbit leg. I pound my head to see if Im goin blind by slight degrees or what. Then just over the rise I see that tiny hut glowin from inside. Like its one a them Chinese lanterns plunked down there like a tump stone. Bit a flutter in the lumination as I get closer tell me theys a man movin his head in there. I see him already in my mind. Workin at his graphs an tables. You ask how I know. I dont know how. Nor why he would be doin such in the middle a the night.

Closer I get the more the light from the hut blank out the sky. I get up to the door hangin open which is almost one whole wall. An there he is just like I imagine. Tall young man. Starch white big collar. Hair tied back neat with a bright blue ribbon. Porin over a density a numbers by lantern light. Big numbers all feverish in squared out little boxes. Fat night moths is flutterin up around the lantern smoke. My does he got a neat hand. Like engravin on a bank note. Pays no attention to me. Shoulders hunched over. Stares out. Licks his lips a bit. Adds a number to a empty box. I know he know Im there. But you cant fluster that kind. He pinch his nose. Looks up at nothin. Then scratches down another number. Like they come out a the air. Like the air be full a secret numbers. Hes bent over his table so at first I cant parse his face. But I knowd it was a man I never seed before. Back then is when things start to change. You count up all the men throughout a day you never seen before an that number be half as much as the men you do know.

Peculiar thing was that lantern hangin high behind his head. His shadow fall square on the page an he have to keep movin back an forth to write them numbers down. Which he did in no particular order or hurry I could figure. Just fillin in the boxes. Thirty nine an ninety five. Sixty seven. Forty four. I see em red an black an edged in gold behind my eyelids. Numbers out a the air. Then he turn an look at me. Like hes been waitin. Flat mild face. Dead eyes. Thin smile not hooked up to the rest of him. When I dont speak he look back down an brush off somethin from the page. Says a curious thing off to his side. Not lookin at me. Its already Sunday as far as we are concerned he says. Precise like that. To hisself maybe. Or someone somewhere else. All a them numbers. Theys somethin there that dont favor us. Come to me I could a killt him right there on the spot. He wouldn a resisted I know that. Just smiled that smile into my knife if thats how Id a done him. Smilin lookin like hes made a the same stuff as that hut. Or I would a choked the air off in his wind pipe get that smile to fade. But I knowd itd just hang there in the dark. Maybe he just vanish in a puff a smoke. But there be another just like him the next day. Then another. Same numbers. Same damn smile.

Look over there. Where Lalloways scrapin her stick against the wall. She run at ya or stay away from ya like a child. Just never growed up. Cept part of hers well aware about the woman inside. An that dont help her none. Like some young girls know all that an flaunt it at you when a righeous lad cant do squat about it. They say Lalloway stop talkin right after seein a man whipped to death an then a dog eat his ear. I dont know. Most ever one see such like things. Over just beyond Lalloway is where that cheese rind hut sat. That become our luminated manufactory so fast you forget what things was like before. Light spill from ever window. Smoke pour from the stacks. Steam hiss from the pressure boxes. Engines clank. Shuttles chatter. No more righteous rest under the stars anywhere near that place.

> *Look you all about you*
> *Through the darkness of the night.*
> *The dawn is always rising*
> *Where the factorys alight*

Withy & Co it say on the big sign board. Except the *W* an *C* is so big it look like *W C* if you squint right. What they call the so called water closets beginnin to be installed. Withys is the first place here abouts to get one cept for the court house. An so first we call the factory Piss Pot an then Shit House.

When them birds stop talkin to me the silence is a desolate thing. Desperate thing. Desolate for me an desperate for them. I didn know if its everbody or theys just not talkin to me. Or if by not talkin to me theys tryin even harder to tell me somethin. Somethin they cant say in their language. I mean tweetin pretty you hear that. But there aint no pungent words no more. I ast Rose Stonewarden if she notice when the birds stop talkin. She says oh Corbel them birds. Big black crow try to take my sack a Iron Seed just yesterday mornin. Had to put a broom to him. He dint get none of it she says. He wouldn go away though. Kept a watch on me all afternoon. You tell em to stop that Corbel she says. Read the Black Book Rosie I want to say to her but I dont. Seven heavens. You cant tell a black crow nothin. I ast Tam Brigby but he was still too shook from Will Flowers hangin. Panks no good. Too much riddle me this riddle me that. So I ast Maggie Moats. Shes not a party to anything. Well Corbel you know she says. The clankin at the factory. The shoutin a the river boys. My laundry flappin in the wind I only got me one good ear an my fool husband Barley stop talkin to me since he come home drunk an broke the back steps an I wouldn carry him in. So I got to listen out special for Barley she says. In case he start up again. Too much rattle any road she says.

So like that. Then one day I spot a greatcoat flasher on a dead branch not lookin at me. So I try to show my sympathy by offerin scrap a rhyme from somewhere.

> *What bird sing but yet doth wail*
> *It be the famished nightingale*

Luck luck luck to you she cry
At midnight clear I hear her sigh

I chirp it out twice but nothin. Then I get glum when I number all the ways a greatcoat flasher might a took offense at my overture. Most folk may think the nightingale she got a special mission. The conference a birds may not agree. One thing though. People has always ast me. Corbel how is it you say you talk to them birds an you cant even name one sort from another. Well I do know this. That dont offend em. If I call it a upright pecker or a regal grabcock or a faded bunting and it truly be a cock swallow or a wagtail trixie or a ringneck bludgeon it dont matter. Birds dont care what you call em an they dont see what you see. It was New Billy who find a big white wing half as tall as him. Chewed off an bloody at the end but pristine as to feathers an extent. Big sea bird most like. Billy start draggin that thing along with him an I ast him where he get it. Knowin it wernt a question with a good answer an probly with no answer or a bad one. I kill the bird that made the breeze to blow he says but without his snarly smile. Wheres he come up with such gobbin.

Things start to happen fast. Pank an me we find a dead man propped up against a tree some ways off the Bastford road with a red spotted hooter shoved down his throat. Beak stickin out between his lips. It may a been a rosy tit. Hard to tell em apart. Pank says to me what you make of it Corbel. I says I think this be a message but I dont know what. Pank finger that hooter or could be tit loose with some delicacy cause the feathers is stuck to the mans lips. Pank says he was a cook doublin as a night guard at Maltby an Briggs. Rumored to be killt by Ludds men. But why would they shove a bird in his mouth I ask him. An John Baal a seedsman out a Warmouth come by one day to sell cauliflower seed to Rose. She plan to grow two plots to cart off an a bed to keep. You pickle them little caul buds with brine vinegar an tiny onions an six snapper pods stuffed down in a crock. Thats a gift in a basket with a couple a pies. But all these John Baal cauls come up black wormy cabbage instead. I hear hes later pinched for seed fraud. Had to pay back in weight an a fine. That black cabbage stink up heaven an you want to stay far away when you cook it. Rose load most of it off at the cow market over to Six Acres. Pigs wouldn even eat that dung wrap. Then you hear about the dogs mercury that rise up showin faces in the leafs like chimney rabble. You start to hear talk a this so called scientific seed. All I know is John Gwilt buy some giant peaches from a man at Mechanick Arts. They do all kind a freakish things up there. Could be this aint dogs mercury but some new thing. Ben Maldon come back from France an find some new weed is chokin out his radishes. He try to pull it up but all the radishes come up with it theys so entangled. You rub your hands on it your fingers smell just like a mans sweet spunk. Somebody call it prickspill an now its here to stay seem like. I always wonder why royal cuntwig or pies eyeball aint the same for ladies. But cuntwig smell like fox grass. Pies eyeball smell like your sour greens lyin in the pot all night. No plant I know convey the essence of a lady twixt her wind an her water. An if they was such the ladies wouldn like it.

Somewhere about this time Rose Stonewardens sister come to stay with her. One day she sidle up to me the way them sisters do an says Mister Penner I have a strong dream last night. Will you take me out to hear them birds talk. I want to tell her I dont know nothin about it. Maybe she be playin me the fool. You cant be certain. A pretty dream its like a ladys basket I says to her. You wont get to the bottom. Oh please Mister Penner take me out she say. So I go ask Rose an she says it be fine with her. Well not so much says that but she dont say not to. So I take her round with me. Two three morns that week I mightn a got up so early cept for her. Though mornins is when the birds is freest with their ponders an equivocations. But it was after noon one day I tell her I got to go to Ben Maldons depot to pick up a couple a iron claw for Withy an do she want to ride along. She do. An after the turn off to Runny Pumps I stop my cart. Warm sun. You can smell the royal cuntwig in the meadow. Clank a someone mendin a wheel across the vale. Some reason the manufactory aint clankin just then. Sometimes the big belt slip off the rotor an they gots to shut the engine. Cloud shadows ripple over the rock. Too quiet. Thats the feelin that come over me. Then I see a yellow flutter an a black flash where a branch is bobbin up an down in a bush. I get the guy good an pointed in the leafage. He jerk his little head an pipe out. *Marie. Marie. May be Marie.* Well Rose sisters name wernt Marie but its a openin. I cross her lips with my finger to shush her. Fellow fly off then but fly right back with a friend just like him. They bounce an skitter there an look about. *Hear me Theresa. Hear me dearie. Hear me Theresa. Hear me dearie.* Well Roses sisters names not Theresa neither its Mildred. But I never ever hear a bird say Mildred. That wont happen.

So I dont know what to think. I try a Swiss whistle what was taught me one night at the Lion by a pair a drunk Zermatt yodelers. That shut them birds right up for a time. Pretending theys not even thinkin about it. Then I try *Say what you will but is it true. Say what you will but is it true.* An soon as I toot that out I knowd it was the word true I shouldn a used. Its a short good word. Sweet an sturdy. You say it without thinkin an you think you know what it mean an ever one agree. But it seem to put em off an things get all quiet again. Think on it. You hear them folk gone south a Bastford that speak with other tongues as the spirit move em. Like the birds you dont understand em but that dont mean it aint true. Im just about to ask Mildred what she make of all this. Its a chance to see if others who dont know nothin of it hear em like I do. But then the first bird blurt out *Eat her here. Eat her here. Eat her eat her here.* An at that very moment I swear Mildred she look up at me an say Mister Penner did you ever see birds kiss. Well no matter what happen now its another mess. Like the time I only try to prop it up but a birds nest fall apart an splatter eggs an twig fluff all in my hair. Aint a lady born dont know how to charge a moment.

Later I hear Rose talkin to Sarah Maldon by the pump in factory square. They dont see me. Oh that Corbel Rose says. Bird in the hand worth ten in the head I do guess. My sister Mildred bless me she swear she hear em talk. Corby take her out. I cant stop her. She come back smilin an wont say no more about it Rose says. You know that Corbel. Rose an Sarah stand there laughin. Rose I dont mind if she laugh at me. Sarah it matter more what she think. Got a higher purpose behind her eye. But Rose prattle on while shes fillin the buckets.

> *There was a old owl lived up in a oak*
> *The more he heard the less he spoke*
> *Until he spoke nary a word*
> *If only that be Corbels bird*

Lookin back on it I cant disagree. But for a while its everbody sayin Mister Penner please take me out to hear the birds talk. When Desmond Carke put on a ladys voice its most annoyin.

I did go pick up a iron claw that day. They was only one not two. Ask George Withy. I brung it to him later an all he do is shout at me. I aint seen a sales man in two month he says. An all you bring me is one iron claw. Well I dont know then that Ben Maldon he put the other aside for his own purposes. Words comin down he says. From Napoleon hisself. There be two hundred French men an fifteen cannon. Catapults. Ready to come over. Old Boney knows Ned Ludd he says. Met with him in secret an he like what he hear. I be goin back to France in two months time Ben says. Ludds men got a plan for the factory smashin they should get the word to me. Now a course I wonder what Ben say he could do would a helped or hurt. Now it seem like the smaller the better is the way things worked for the Iron Boys.

Dont like to mention numbers. Start up with em an they can worm their way under the flap a your cap an infect your thinkin. Im always countin. When the birds stop talkin to me I start countin even more. Use to count steps mostly when I had my walkin legs. I can tell you how many steps to Bell Misty. How many steps to Peterlawn. Least ways to where them towns be when they had a center or an edge. Now new roads is goin here an there an not always on the straight an narrow. Theres inclosures. Any man with a barrowll be hired to cart off boundary stones to build some wall somewhere else. Town grow out new lines on you. How many steps round Robin Hoods barn. No one know that. Hard to keep your count straight. Some says they want it that way. Taxation an what not. But I warn you. I tell you bout numbers an youll come to curse me on it. It just start your fingers tappin over everthing. There be no end to it. You watch if it dont be like a itchy cloak. Numbers everwhere. All over maps. Years. Price a lace in China. How old are you. Population. How many got the French pox. Numbers boilin on the surface of a burblin spring. Our Iron Boy twistin ins is numbered. Men in prison is numberin their days. But you dont get to a million that way. I remember the day Withy hes all crowin about a million. Never did find out a million a what though. But you an me an the blood on the wall we be one by one by one by one an who gots a million a anything. Aint no end to numbers.

I dont suppose there never were no use to all that countin. Though me Id love to go some day an number off my old paths once again. But how would I count without my legs. They tell me all the ways is growin shorter with more people in the world. Or it may be all them new folks legs is gettin longer. *Ten thousand steps to Unicorn Bridge.* That aint no simple proverb like you think. I mean its right on the button. I counted it. Ten thousand steps an not a half shuffle more from Hog Top dribble to where Unicorn Bridge sign post use to be. Hog Top dribble it aint there no more neither. Dried up when they put the culvert in. I get into a fight with Pank House over it. This is just before Ise twisted in to the Iron Boys. Some reason I says it to him. I dont know why. Like you might say *This road go both ways.* Or *You cant get there from here.* Aint nothin more than that. But I knowd he would take offense. *Ten thousand steps to Unicorn Bridge* I says. Pank roll his big superior eyeballs over me like Ise a child. Though Ise older than him even in those days. Scrape that poop off your boots he says. Stop spreadin that unicorn shit. You best save them ten thousand steps. You be needin em. Well I been there I says. Thats all I says to him. Dont mean nothin by it. I didn say I seen the bridge. He spits an scuffs it in the dirt. You might as well be drunk all day from sniffin Marys honey oyster while they steal your boots. I come to tell you Corbel in this world they tie your ankles to the lanyard an run you up a flag pole. That shit sweet manufactory smoke he says. You like to smell it but it aint your mornin rum soaked pipe weed. Its from your great grease engines everwhere. They feedin them machines he says. An them sacks a feed is you an me. Now your handsll be too busy to be curled around your ding dong dilly. I cant help myself. I seen where that bridge use to be I says. You must a seed it too I says. You go up to Feathermarket you cant miss it. Aint hardly nothin there no more but a square hole in the stone where the sign post was I says. An the land tumble down to the pebble bed where the creek use to be. Ten thousand foot slaps. Straight as a noon pint I swear. From Hog Top dribble right that way through the hole in the hedge I says to Pank. Course they aint no hole in the hedge neither. Aint no hedge. An what Im pointin at is Withys manufactory like it seem you do when you point anywhere nowdays. Which demonstrate Panks meanin an he dont need to say so. Well I do know what youre talkin bout Corbel he says. I surely do. Now Panks eyes look sad. Cause he think he has to let me down easy. Like whys this growed up fellow givin me the fairy glim. He says to me I know youre talkin bout the virgin an the ruby. Well Corbel I been all about. An ever place thats bigger than a pile a cow flop with a stick in it they tell the same story. You got your blind virgin. You pry the ruby from a unicorns horn which restore her sight an she marry you because youre the prince. You hear the same thing in Raw Morton he says. Spindleford. You even hear it over in French Town. An what do you know. You cant find a Unicorn Bridge in any a them places.

But I dont care shit about what Pank think. I know I been to where it was at least. An if theys a Unicorn Bridge I figure theys unicorns once about. Ten thousand steps exact from right over there. I count em twice goin an once back. Course I suppose you adjust your gait if your totals comin up over or under what you know it should be. But I hit ten thousand ever time. What difference is it if you hear the story everwhere. Seem to me thats a argument in favor. So I says to him Im sure to ponder that. But I ast him wont he tell me more about the twistin ins. Knowin he wont but it move him on to some other thing. We already get a whiff from the *Notifier* when they print Ned Ludds oathin letter. What they hang them boys for over to Macclesfield. Top a the page. Framed in death edge black. I know two three folk tear it up or burn it to keep from bein taint. Ever one afraid to even mumble it. Not me. I know that aint the true story. True story dont get put at the top a the page. This were like a hook you dangle at the sunny end a the pond. Or as a threat it work all right. But I learnt it any road. Might find a use for it. Might be good to know.

> *I hereby freely declare and solemnly swear*
> *I will never reveal to any mortal*
> *the name of any brother or sister*
> *marching in the army of King Ludd.*
> *I will not aver nor avow aught of our methods*
> *our orders our meetings our missions*
> *our homes or disguises or signs*
> *or any other such thing.*
> *Under penalty of swift departure from this world*
> *before I am ready at the true end of a knife.*
> *My name to be blackened and burnt thereafter*
> *and my honest memory forever scorned by all.*
> *Further do I swear that I shall not rest*
> *until I deliver unto death*
> *by virtue of this oath of grue*
> *all traitors to our cause*
> *forever to the edge of doom.*
> *Sworn this day by solemn Oath*
> *and blood red Sign*

But I was speakin bout the numbers. How they come to fill my head. May a started with that tallow fellow in the hut. Fillin in his spider grid by lune light. I still wonder if I should a killt him. But at the time it wernt like me. That came later. Soon after the pig line race at the fair there be lots a fine folk hitherin an thitherin. Lot a your official sort what stand around an point an jaw an wave their arms an stab their quills to make occasion. Testin the weather. Frownin over your shoulder. Lookin at the clouds. Steppin back an forth across them cords. Withy he stalk about an weave his plans in an out amongst em. It all concern the buildin of his manufactory. Though few back then was clear on what that portend. Someone decide they gots to move the old mill pond. Why. You tell me an one of usll know. But move it they would an move it they did. Lot a calculatin over it. Pocky man in a black city coat he ast me in his puffed up way. How big sir would you say is this mill pond. I mean sir when compared sir he says with the similar pond at Westhoughton. His be the kind a sir that make you want to slap him three times quick like Frenchmen do. I slide the question straight back at him. Whose poxy mother need this information I say. Well sir he says we have made our most precise an folderol an farrago an such like calculations. We would most appreciate your own esteemed an worthless opinion in this coster monger calabash et cetera so to speak.

Im about to prank up a birdish sort a reply but as Im lookin at him numbers swim up sharp behind my eyes. One an two an four an five an seven bobbin in an out. But lookin permanent. Like bank note figures. Bout three fifth I says to him. He raise his eye brows under his tall hat. Three fifth. Three fifth. He hawks an hmms. His eyes is flittin an his lips is pinchin an he look like my number put him on one side of a wager an not the right side neither. Now pray sir Mister Black Coat says. Would that three fifth be your plumb line proximation of depth or your median diameter or your very own footly circumference. Is your figure sir reflecting cubic volume or capacity of flow. Well I didn reply. Such humber bumber keep a blind owl awake all night. An that word cubic burn me good an proper. So I just skip a stone across the long way. It hop three times. I once did five across Westhoughton Pond I says to him. Thats what they call it. Be the same one we call Pond Over. Most times I do only four. It depend. On what he says. On the wind I says. The weir. The stone. My arm. The angle of the dangle on your mamas cubic backside. May them numbers be more helpful to you sir.

What I wouldn tell him is a truer thing about the size a water. You walk around that pond. Any pond. Dont count your steps. Look at your reflection at the big end an the small end. Sunny day an cloudy day. Summer fall winter spring. Bright dawn an moonless night. Flat noon. Row yourself across an back. May be once you done got thowd in by bad boys. An then you hear the stories a who drownded there. Thats how you tell the size a that pond. Aint no numbers to it. Any road the new mill pond is dug out in a hurry. Ever since its always been a tiddly pond. Dont run right. Get a shiver on it on a still day make you back away some times. Like a wet dog shake hisself right underneath. Couldn get them numbers out a my head. Three fifth. Three fifth. I didn even know what I was sayin but that three an that five I can see em with the line between em that Miss Bird drawed in chalk to show us fractions. Whatever they is. Couldn say what that line mean though I once thought I knowd an I still think I do. An when ever I set my face to water. Down at the dribblin brook or when the pump splash out. Them numbers roll around an show up inside my eyes. They come out a the water like. Nine nine six seven. Thirteen sixty eight four two. Eleventy nine fourteen eight an six. Five five three an forty one. On an on an on. Well thats just me. I mean one two three four five six seven eight nine thats always goin on I guess.

So the numbers move in over us. We Iron Boys even take em at our twistin ins. Each one get a number. Thats what we knowd each other by. All thats forgotten now. Cept for old Forty Four who dont seem to remember nothin else. He still wont have no other name. Still proud a number Forty Four an what it signify though he dint do nothin with it. Four an Forty. Thats all you get from him. Even now you want to poke him in the belly with a stick. No mam he always say. Man or woman it dont matter. No mam. Four an Forty. Thats all you get from me he says. That be my name. No one ever find me out. Number Forty Four. It got significance dont you think. Ise an old man now. Well I dont need to tell you that he says. On my tombstone it be just the same he says. Forty Four in curly figures just like that. Would a had it needled on my skin he says. That times not yet they tells me. My stones carved already waitin he says. Well not stone but wood carved an painted up to be like marble in the graveyard dark. What I could pay for. Well they pay me back if I can sell twelve more stones before my time he says. Already sold two. Forty Four. Beautiful. Run your thumb along the edge he says. He close his eyes an curl his fingers as if hes feelin it right there in front a me. Big numbers with the little tails he says. Sharp corners keep em good an edgy when they get wore down. Even your hard stone wash out blank in time he says. Angel trumpets on either side he says. Beautiful I dont mind tellin you. Though aint no pride amongst the dead no mam. Bones is bones he says. Those visitin the pious bone yardll see me number there an wonder on it. Puzzle an perhaps admire. An me be down there under em he says. I been told the dead they shrink like cloth on the bleachin field. I dont think thats true.

You hear what happen to John Gwilt he says. He once dig a hole an come upon a iron coffin seven cubits long. John bury it again without lookin in it. Afraid to see the giants bones I guess he was. Some nights he says I look up an cant see nothin. An I think Im under ground already. Forty Four he grab my arm. Can you see me here he says. Do you think Im under. Do you see me. Would you pinch me. Go an see my stone he says. Though its made a wood. Its over Little Glossop Street behind the breakers. Ask for Conny Farthing. He show you. Will Flowers stone come from there too he says. I sell that stone to Wills sister. Actual stone he get. I tell his sister exactly what to carve.

> *Will Flowers "63"*
> *Plays the heavenly lyre*
> *Born bred & hanged*
> *All in the same shire*

She didn think it right at first. I dont know. To me it have a nice ringy ring to it. An ever word be true. We Iron Boys we will not be forgot he says. Will Flowers. Only fifteen year. Too young to make any lass a widow any road. There it is for all to see. Under the spreadin chestnut tree. Forty Four is all you get from me. God go with you mam he says. Fours the blessed number. It be square an Forty Fours a double square I guess. God hisself dont need no more to call me to the gates but Forty Four. I take the Iron Boy oath not knowin what it is. Forty Four. Thats the end. I say no more he says. The devil on his rearin horse get nothin else from me an why should you he says. Well you cant long mimic Forty Four without a chuckle. All he live for now is what loom over him when hes dead. He wont let you alone about it. Pank once says to me. That Forty Four he says. He need a clock in his coffin. So he know when its time to stop talkin. Forty Four be a clear example. Numbers claim us all now days one way an another.

YOU KNOW THEM BIRDS

You know them birds ast me a question once. *Why dig down. Search sweet air. Why dig down. Search sweet air.* I suppose thats the avian alternative. Wisht I wernt alone in hearin it. Would a liked Forty Fours view of it. Would a liked Rose Stonewardens too. She spend all her time these days movin rocks back an forth in her garden. Well thats her name I guess. An Maggie Moats diggin that well with no help from Barley. *Why dig down.* Aint no swift answer to it. Question shake itself at you like a diggin dog. Could be it aint even a question. Tried to talk back to the little guy but he just whistle up another taunt. *Witchery witchery which way sir.* Which way indeed. Aint hard to laugh at Forty Four. But you know I wish sometime I got a numbered stone to mark my legs when they was cut from me. Course we got no sanction to tell our Iron Boy numbers. Forty Four. Sixty Three. Guess the oath dont mean much. But I aint tellin mine. They cut my legs off here just above the knee. I seed em lyin beside me. They show em to me on the slab or else I dreamed it. Thems walkin nowhere no more. They just thew em in a ditch with the other hospital trash that day. I could a put em in half a coffin. Have half a stone carved to bury em under. Put half a number on it. Write half a poem to em.

Corbel Penner
Walks no more

Thats the half I got so far. What should I say to my legs now. What would they say back.

Winter come. Some year got some number on it. Im prepared. Got my horse Gladden an my cart for haulin. Got my legs then too. Build me a little cabin on the cart back. My coffin cart Pank call it but its enough to sit up in. Inside nice nooks an notches ranged around to hold the necessaries. Water skin an dram flagon tied up tight above my head. Got a strap basket for hard meat. Mesh sack strung for apples. Nails to hang the cheese. Bread dont stay round long enough to need a special place. Riggin in the roofll hold the lantern. Covered spout to spill the exhalations an keep out the cold drips. Bag a meadow bells to rest my head an remind me a Silvy.

One December night. Wind pick up flappin though the sky is clear as Christmas bells. Soon rains flailin about wild. Crashin straight down from upper heaven though I can still see some stars. Im urgin Gladden along the back way to Golspie but the track is muddin up fast. My wheels is slippin. Its near enough Brindles bake house to unhitch an run Gladden on into the barn. She get on good with Brindles horses. Chock my cart off against the back oven wall. Itll get too hot come first bake but right now theys a hairy blow comin on so you want a wall. Its eerie though since the sky keep a comin onyx clear in patches. So Im in the barn there with Gladden an Oatsy an Muslin. I shovel em up a heap a bakin straw. I like to be with em cause I can tell things I wouldn know elsewise. But Im wonderin where Brindles at. He always take good care a things. Soon there come a dire bangin outside cant be good. Like a bitter old thing want release but wont accept it. Like Great Mam when she stump her cane on the floor with a no tooth frown an wont say why.

There be a old demon who live in her dress
Flutter her unders an maketh her mess

So I walk out leanin hard against the wind across the yard to Brindles front door. Which is slammin back an forth fair to bring the whole house down. It bang open an I think I see a torch movin round inside. Fluttery change a shadows any way. I get me a stick to push ahead with. Devil can set a brick house on fire in this wind. Just as Ise about to stab through the door way a man in a cape an hood stride out like Death Be Nimble. Sack over his shoulder slung full a long loafs. B for Brindle branded on ever end stickin out a the sack. Must be left from mornin bake. He pull out a loaf an hand me it with a slow nod like either him or Ise the one who knows. Then he walk off into the wind with his cape flappin out behind. Im certain I never seed him before. Inside the Brindles is gone. Fire dead. Food scraps greasy on the table. I cant stay to look at that cold empty place. Rain let up for now but still the weird wind. I go back to the shed for Gladden. Knowin she wont want to leave her friends an shelter for such a fraught night on the road. But she be by herself in there lookin at me fright eyed from the corner. Oatsy an Muslin is circlin in opposite directions.

Half way on to Golspie the wind die down a bit. I see a big wet pile a somethin side the road. Come to be Joad an Sissy Brindle an their children. Two three I dont remember. An theys heaped up what they carry an tied blankets over it all. Aye Joad I says. Man aint long gone fore his house is wide open an makeshift devils take off with his bread. That aint no more my house he says. Aye Joad I says. Oatsy an Muslin they be left there trampin. Terrified a Gladden like never pass before. Those no more be my horses he says. Well. What the wind dont chill a mans words will. I see then an there that that be that. Joad aint even lookin at me. Next day that storms all blowed off. An no one never see nothin a the Brindles again. I realize two things. Folks you know middlin well can up an disappear for good. They be a reason but you cant always know what it is. Things change but when do it begin.

I had a friend named Eddard Weedy. Could be I seed him only eight ten times in all but must a been enough to make it stick. I see Withy an John Gwilt ever day. Pank House two three times a week. Yet somehow I aint so close to them as to Eddard an he aint around no more. Even so I feel like I should say I have a friend. I called him Teddy. Knowd of him fore I meet him. Desmond Carke was sloppin it up one night at the Lion. I run into a odd fellow Desmond says. Up High Bascombe way. Name a Weedy an weedys what hes like. Playin cards without a table at the Ha Ha Club. Desmond quote him in a mockin voice.

Alexanders royal rod
Be the bridge from man to god

Then he put his hands over his ears. You wouldn believe a man could say such shit an sit there pole face like that he says. I can tell Desmonds offended by what be larger than his understandin. Somethin tell me then an there that I would meet this Eddard Weedy. An true to tell I find him without tryin. Mostly he stay up past the trottin tracks at Dutch Town. Or even out beyond Badgery Beacon. He wernt one to come to you. But we fall in with one another like. Like what. Weed brothers. Bird brothers. Brothers from the war. One day on the road to Golspie there he is. Hes always one step ahead but not pullin you anywhere. He always knowd right where I am in my mind. We sit up top Wise Crag to watch the stars a night or two. Stars was Teddys guide. Navigatin inside like. He point out the big W up there. Some say thats Queen Cassie tipped back on her throne he says. But in truth that W stand for Weedy. My celestial forebears on my mothers side. Then he sketch out Orion an his club an sword. An Arthurs Coffin which circle close around the pole star. Teddy know the names a all the stars that make up Arthurs sky box. Or some call it Great Bear or Thigh a the Bull though it dont look like none a them things. I can still say the names a them stars. Mirak. Phekda. Megrez. Alioth. Mizar. Sound like a Turkish oath I reckon. An the magistrates be afraid a all the Luddite oathin. Well there could be worse hedgehoggery up there in the black. Zubenelgenubi. Thats over in another part a the sky. Make you chuckle just to say it. I tell Teddy I like the sound a that one. Thats where youre from he says. I guess cause Ise born in October. Zubenelgenubi. Whod believe it. Seeds Teddy says. Seeds in the sky. Look up there. Thats what seeds in the earth is like unto themselves. Them stars is nearer to you than you think he says. I tell you Teddys head was right up there. But his roots go all the way down. You can see it in his eyes when he look at you good. Which is not often.

Any road one time him an mes talkin in some dark Dutch Town inn. Things is in the air. Some loom smashins that week round about. Withyd been conversin with the magistrate an there was guards put on the factory. All our private whispers concern the Iron Seed. Mean time it was iron winter. I believe Will Flowers hant yet been hung. So must be February. Spitters an speechifiers come round on the roads. I recall one such rouse em good. Give em what they come to hear. Straw has thorns an thy pay keep sinkin he says. Thy bucket have a sip an they drink it. Thy bucket have a drip an they dry it. Thy bucket hang empty an they cut the bottom out. Brothers an sisters is arisin from vale an moor he says. Here to Saint Cuthberts. Bell Misty. Spindleford. I seen em. You seen em. No new work in the mills. Take up the wandern life bag an nag. Aint ever be so many on the roads before he says. Nothin much to grub on. Land a comin restless. Dead things walkin about. Ghosts in the valley ready for somethin he says. Are you ready he says. Are you ready to testify. An some of em is ready. But for what. Im tellin all this to Teddy. Tryin to glean his view. No one understand the blockade. What it mean. War in France. Power looms producin too much goods with too few hands. Ben Maldon an his traipsin to the coast an cross the channel. Smugglin an the so called shadow markets. Im tryin to put it all together. Teddy hear me out till Im stumped in thick confusion. As we all was in those days.

Loom he says an puts a tubish curl around the word. He lick his fingers an run em back to tuck his hair behind his pointy ear tips. It remind you of a bird somehow even though aint no bird would do that even if they could. Which they cant. Prior to the current disputations he says. Loomin dark an mighty as machines jeer at us all. The word loom in times of old it mean many differnt things. Such is its dark potency an power to confuse. A loom could be a tub or vat or pot for grain or beer he says. Could be a axe or rake or tool of any kind. An under such a heading come your weapons.

> *Glinting lances are the loom*
> *Weaving many a soldiers doom*

Or as great Percival told it *I make my loom of hornbeam an with such a loom I fight.* But tool as all men know he says and women to a fare the well it hath a deeper meaning. So of great Alexander this was sung.

> *Huge was his odd loom*
> *The length of most a yard*

Loom me he says an fetch up a deep chuckle without a smile on top. Indeed he look most serious. Poor Alexanders sweet heir loom he says. That most utile though sadly shriveled rod survives unto this day. Preserved with unguents from the orient east. Wrapped in roebuck hide cut from Dianas sacred gambeson. Handed secretly from man to man he says across the so called generations. Teddy nod a sage nod an fix his hats position an clear his throat most thoroughly. Alexanders noble rod he says has been a wand for a magus here an there an cultish worship through the years. An in the reign of Old Cole who wernt a king by the by it commonly serve other ends he says.

That Gods may view
With a dildo do
What we bake
An what we brew

How be it that you know all this I must have ast at some point. But you get nowhere by askin.

We was silent for a time. Theres some more he says. You wont know this Corbel with your fear a water. A loom be part a the handle of a oar. That very part without another name you always wonder about. An loom is what the sailors call the guillemot. The famous divin bird. Black up top an snow white on the belly. So says the narrative of Ross whose crew survived the arctic winter on loom soup. You start to see the layerin he says. An further off from shore he says there looms the hazy spot where land come into view. The spot where theres no trust in what you see. An the loomin of the ocean is that catback motion up an down. Well he says. Now you see the challenge. If words mean what they say then there looms here a missin link. Just as your manufactory frame is linked on one hand to the steam box an on the other to the threads wove up in many differnt colors. All this may a took Teddy most of a day to tell. He unwind it slow with much between. Like you unwind your bird line through the trees. In angles so they dont know where you been.

Then there was our walk to Golspie. Must be April. Two days amble. No good reason. Just to do it. I make up some business I can go check on. Teddy though I think his mothers there abouts though he never so much say so. We been dry ploddin on a while. Pass a big bush where there come a huge flappin racket out the thick of it. Which startle me as I was drenched in thought about the loomin a the sea. I seen it once upon a time as a lost lad wonderin whats to become a me. An Im wonderin how Teddy know my feelins about water. Then slap slap slap slap quick. Them birds wings hittin so hard against their little bodies. They must hurt themselves. Is they irritated or stupid I cant say. Just then Eddard made a backward shuffle an a hop. He jump the ditch an take his hat off. Start a conversation with a claycheek plough boy workin there. An soon enough they has their pants down like to like an Eddard spread him strong between the rows. Trousers bunched down around their knees. I aint lookin though your eye cant help noticin the bouncin motion where aint nothin else move for days. An then theys up an Eddard clasp the fellow both hands round the shoulders. He kiss him sweet there on the lips an then slide down him like a swoon. He slip somethin in the plough boys palm an scramble back aside me on the road. As if nothin. I think I must a knowd he wernt shank with the ladies. So I ast him why he do that like that. Keep the clouds out a my eyes he says. Keep the stars clear in the sky.

That night we reach a deft place up a grassy rise. Everythings drawed in. Clouds hang drear an low. We bundle down against the night between a hay rick an a fence. Teddy measure his words like hes prepared em. I should be a fierce astronomer he says. King of a cruel an far flung empire. Ruthless in my quest for high dry land an long clear nights. Spendin all my fortune for the right view a the heavens. Thats a sight for very few he says. Most folk you cant make em look up at the stars. Like tryin to make a dog look in a mirror. If I had been on gods left hand in creation days instead a that other fellow he says Id a given god some hints for better orderin the universe. Then Teddy shuts his eyes an soon he start to snore. That was the only time I ever hear him speak a anything with such a governmental bent. I had to think upon it. That he might dragoon folk into watchin stars as was our pleasure. Well aint one thing with Teddy were a simple thing.

Hangin over that year is the comet. Cant never forget that. It first appear in that cold spring. Biggest comet ever seen Weedy says. That should tell you somethin. Aint but a smudge in the sky at first. I make nothin of it but I dont see so good. Theys some talk in the square. Misfigured lambs an blight in the comin crop. Bad twins. The fortunes a Napoleon. One crystal night it seem all close at once. I can see a blood red tail brushed out like feather malt. Wide an tall an just that spiky. Weedy says it were a Frenchman spot it first. Out a their froggy pride they drum up all the virtues a their comet wine. Best vintage for twenty annos so they say. If we had seen it first no doubt our tapsters here would be singin comet stout. What we did have that autumn is the fattest sweetest penny lucre melon you ever taste. Too sweet an ponderous for me. Ladies sport the special melon bibs that fall. Soak up all the juice what other wise would run indecorous down their dainty chinny chins. No one never needed melon bibs before but Withys quick to make em out a scraps.

Young lad wander in from Child Town. No doubt they can see the comet better. No factory lights out there. Whats it mean. Why dont it go away the little fellow says. Eddard Weedys brung along a telescope he set up on three sticks. Folk come by to have a look. Mary Lake wont. The more you look at it the longer itll stay she says. I skrinch my eye up to the glass. Stringy milky blob. You dont see the whole extent of it at once. Which seem a disadvantage to magnifyin things. Couldn do much about it right then. Later it come to visit me in a dream. Its just about to loom there in the circle a the scope but wont come into view. Im fightin with them sticks in my dream to try an point em right. Dang if my hand aint sore when I wake up. Child Town lads transfixed though. He wont let Eddard take the spyglass down. Whats your name son Eddard says. Milky the lad says lookin at the ground. Milky thats a curious name Eddard kindly says. My sister give it to me he says. Cause I always ask for milk. Eddard draw his finger cross a inch a sky. Comet only move a little bit from night to night he says. But that one bits a million miles. Milkys eyes an mouths wide open. I can see it move he says. Me an Teddy smile. Cause it dont move like that. But you know how a child will say a thing even though he know it aint true. Teddy says the comet it be naught but icy rock an dust. Dust strewn along like glowin seed. Itll fade he says. Youll forget it in the spring. An that did happen.

Meantime a pack a troubled folk follow a barreltop preacher out a town. Coal sacker an his wifes the only ones I knowd. Oliver Gillham an Sally. Bind their clothin up inside other clothin an move on. Smilin they was. Fire in the eye. Their lodgin in Pruitts Yard is taken the next day. You best heed the signs in the sky Oliver warn me fore he go. As if signs is lackin anywhere. I learn more from watchin a icicle drip from the corner a my cart roof than from any dozen issues a the *Notifier*. Signs dont always speak straight neither. Old sign on a post back a Nancys place. Dont feed sick horse it says. Wernt no horse there that I knowd of sick or no. But that sign stay there forever. Meanin somethin I suppose to someone. This comet now. Aint hard to see its signs if yous wantin to. Arm holdin out a sword. Yeah I seen that. Veins pumped up with the anger a righteousness. Could be I seed that in the telescope. Seven severed heads with briskin beards I dont know. Rose Stonewarden point em out but I couldn see em. But it do fade an we do forget. By then theys too many other things. Comet got no more to teach by such garish signs. But now we Iron Boys was gonna charm a change. Magnetize the seeds like your compass needles. Sow em in the monthly dark. Plant em deep to keep the birds from eatin em. Birds know too much already. Time may come when Iron Boy seedsll bloom an come to fruit an take on new directions from the blackness down below. Eddard Weedy say seeds is mirrored up above. He say therell come a time when ever fallen angle will be made upright. The turn of a five sided wheel it aint smooth but it do turn.

I ast Pank what about them seeds. Even if the Iron Boy seeds is blessed in the bag by moon light. What become of em an why is we involved with it. No one tell me nothin clear I says to him. Pank spits an lowers hisself onto the bucket he just kick off his foot after steppin in it on his way down the ladder from where hes been spyin on somethin. He look me in the eye an says to me. Corbel he says. I always thought a you as one a the ones. One a the what ones I says. Let me try you out on this he says. Let me ask you this. Why is it if a man be cut deep with a bronze blade the wound heal faster than if he be cut just the same with a iron one. Some say bronze is sharper anll cut the flesh like butter he says. You can tell from the blood oozin out swift an clean. But good ironll take the same edge. Iron I think must got a special purpose on the earth.

Let me tell you this Pank says. They be a man once. Hes sittin all alone by the sea shore. I know you never been there Corbel. But try to think of it he says. I squinch my eyes down a little to look like Im thinkin. Dont see no reason to tell him what I know about the sea shore though I cant say sure an dur if it be a memory or a deep sowed iron dream. Pank says many people come up to this man who just want to be alone to aks him shit or importune him. So to get away he row hisself out in the water which is shallow a long way out an he sit there in the row boat lookin at em. An sittin there in the sun after a while he start to talk about this an that. Mostly it be those whos standin near by in the water who hear him. This is what he said says Pank.

There was a fellow with a sack a seed who set off across a field. Its tiny little Iron Seed so as he cast it little bunches fall by the way as he go up an down the rows. First thing is the birds come down an eat their fill. Some a whats left over it fall on stony places. Come sproutin time them sprouts grow quick an tall but rootless cause there aint no deepness to that earth. An later when the sun shine hard upon em them shoots is scorched an withered cause they got no roots in the dark below to cool em. I says to Pank that be like when you run up a stair case an then take one more step which aint there. Then the man sittin in the row boat he say this Pank says. Some a them wayward seed fall in the midst a thorns which choke em off an mangle em. Seed which fall on good black iron soil bring forth good fruit. Whether it be a hunnerd fold or sixty fold or thirty fold. Then Pank says that man in the row boat stand up an shout. *Who hath ears to hear well I say let him hear.*

He roar it out with such force Pank says it set the row boat to rockin an he have to lift his heavy robes an shimmy em about to keep from fallin in the drink. An them who is near Pank says an hath them ears to hear an so can hear him an aks him shit is his minions or his votaries numberin ten or twelve. They kick an slap an stir up the water an shout. An they say to the man in the row boat why are you tellin us stories about seeds. We got no seeds. Ah but you do got seeds the man say back to em. Each an every one a you. An because you got seeds but dont know it you understand me differnt from the others. Then the man in the row boat he tell em of another thing Pank says. Though this time hes sittin down again an not shoutin. The enemy of whom we shall not speak the name the man in the row boat says. He sneak up an sprinkle seeds a that tough yellow daggerweed in between the slender shafts a good brown wheat. In no time the blades a daggerweed has sprung up just as high as the wheat. You try an tear em with your teeth they slit your tender tongue. You can split em stalkwise cept that just double em. He says the seedsman he look at the daggerweed amongst his wheat. His landsmen they ask him should we cut down the enemy weed but he says no. For as you gather up the daggerweed you uproot the wheat also. Let both grow together until harvest time. Then the reapers can gather up the daggerweed an bind it for burnin. An then you can bring the wheat on into my barn. The kingdom of heaven is like to a grain a Iron Seed the man in the row boat says. Which look to be the least of all seeds. Black an hard an barren. But when its growed it is the greatest among herbs and becometh a iron tree an the birds of the air come an lodge in the branches thereof. An Iron Apples come forth and profligate the earth. Thats what the man in the row boat say or so Pank tell me.

Pank look up at me right about then an I realize he aint been lookin at me this whole time. But now his eyes is big an brown an black an wet an shinin an he says to me Corbel I dont know what else I can tell you if that aint clear. Its clear Im thinkin. Clear as dumb slick mud full a pebbles caked up in a horse shoe. I just give him a nod an a wink. Whats clear as the rhyme on a tombstone until it fade out is this. Key to the riddle is them numbers. Hundred fold or sixty fold or thirty fold. Look how they go down instead a up. Unlike Withys ever increasin factory numbers. What this man in the row boats talkin bout may be more like a squirrel pushin a hunker nut too big for him to get his teeth around. Inside that hard green skin like leather you got the nut case. You still aint got the nut. Widow Dedoray showed me a nut shell made into a trinket box with a gold hinge an a clasp too little for your fingers. Wouldn show me whats inside though. Wouldn even let Silvy touch it. Only inside the nut case do you get to the nut all folded in to its nut paper. How do the squirrel know that. I wouldn know it myself if someone didn show me. You cant crack that hard green skin even with a flat hammer. An if you gouge it with a awl the juicell stain you real good. This squirrel I watch him roll that hunker nut with his nose across the dirt into a big bush. I couldn help but laugh. Whats he gonna do with it.

Numbers everwhere. Well it may be the Iron Seed get magnetized to protect itself. Them witchy iron swirls Pank show me could be like the lobes a the hunker nut inside the nut case. Hunnerd. Sixty. Thirty. I keep sayin it over an over on my tongue just loud enough for no one to hear me. Like if I done it long enough it would tell me somethin. Is it some Black Book thing I wonder. What come next. Twenty. Twelve. Ten. Six. Five. Three. Two. One. Thems the only steps I can think of. Where else can it go. An after one come what. It aint gonna be nil cause that be a slidy hole. An it aint gonna be any a them fractions with the lines between. Three fifth like I was sayin at the mill pond. May be what the man in the row boat is sayin is uncalculate them numbers till they come to rest. For what is numbers. An how can there be less than one. The smallest thing an biggest thing is always one.

Well threadless you get born an threadless you be laid out cold is what they tell you. Even if they do dress you up in Withys finery for the pit they drop your box into. Roll me over there into the shade will you. Some times I do wish I aint been borne alive in this age a men. Either died before the Iron Boys or born later like young ones now growin up who never hear of em. Cause the Iron Boy time it come an then it up an go. It did its doin. Now whatever grow out a our Iron Seed yet be far off. Now the grip is in the land like thwacks or the medusa vine. An thats the end. End a the age. Our end any way. Our age. All we can do. Clearer I cant be cause a the mist that grow round everthing year to year. We brung on the storm an it have a greater fury for bein sooner than its time. All round us now is the age a iron. We said yes. We brung it on. We didn know what we was doin. But knowin dont do you no good. Id rather not know. Now you look round its clankin work an woe all day. Fear an flattery all night. Day an night go round like wheels in the machines. The people go round like that too. An work aint naught but worry. As true for all the Withys a the world as for their hirelings. Not for me. Im long gone a that. Got my own place now. No more a my always movin movin movin here an there. Here an there.

Start to make you not know where here is. Not this valley but the world.

Gods green fields springin one from another is now chained more an more by fences. An age mixed up like this got good an evil twinned right down into the smallest particle. Could be thats the so called atom this fellow Johnny Dalton from Cockermouth is speakin of. The smallest thing. Though it come in differnt weights like your shot an your cannon ball. Johnny Daltons father hes a weaver cant barely keep his children in rags. Teddy tell me Johnny write a book. Somethin belike the force a steam at differnt temperatures an the expansion a gas by heat. Could a come straight from Mechanick Arts and pumped right in to Withys. Johnny also keep a weather diary for sixty years an as Teddy says whats the use a that. Weathers gonna change an whats the good in writin it down. Unless a course yous recordin facts like the wind blowin right out your arse. Any road Teddy tell how this Johnny Dalton be ravin about how iron be hard in our files an razors but soft in our horseshoe nails. Which in Denmark he says a smith reject unless he can bend em on his forehead. How with iron we cut an shape iron. How iron it can shatter like glass with a strong arm blow or bend like copper flanges with a pincer twist. How itll melt or refuse to melt. How itll magnetize or refuse to magnetize. Contrary as old Barley Moats. Seem like we dont know what iron is. For beef you can substitute pig or boar. Wool you can replace with cotton or Withys silkeen cloth. If the earth had no iron we couldn make do with another metal. It make you think a the Iron Sermon. Mankind who needeth iron be placed upon a globe filled with it. The least thing an the great be bound together. What more proof need you then of gods design. Course no one ever seed an atom I dont think. So how do they know. Some a this come from Pank who even hear Johnny Dalton speak once up in Manchester or so he says.

But all this busy buildin itll come to an end some day sure an dur. Already I seen a baby born with gray hair down to his little pink behind. His face saggin like a old mans face. Rose Stonewardens sisters child. Mildred. I tell you about her. Wanted to hear the birds. Its her child. By who she wont say. I seen him lookin out a his first eyes an you can tell. He know all about it. Old man inside that tiny pink skin. So old he know that might is all there be to justice when folk lift him up an pinch an slobber on him. He close his little fists to beat against the world with rage an shame an screwed up eyes. I looks at him while Mildred hold his wrinkled body out to me in pride an fear. I didn want to touch him but for his mamas sake I do. Even kings have trepidated at the mortal cry of a marked infant carried in a basket. William Dogg the poet was like to utter such high tone words like out of a book. An if you didn write em down theyd be forgot cause he dont even listen to hisself. Cityll hate city Dogg says.

Mightll be justice an shamell no longer exist. Soresll not heal he says. Only the grabbin machineryll hold things together. The meanll knock down the innocent by sneakin quick chops at the backs a their knees. The wickedll trample the necks a the good Dogg says an whisper sweet lies in their ears like cooin to babes who resist no candied tongue. An birdsll speak only in dulcet diffusions an no longer warn men by their swift auspices. Envyll be a servant to every man an the cost of each egg an bucket a milkll continue to rise an where be the limit for those whose first love is numbers in rut I ask you says Dogg. Youll see faces you love full a hate. Men rejoicin in evil without knowin why. Numbers be branded into the flesh. Honorll vanish Dogg says an no way to hold up your hands to ward it all off. Yet it still be a mixture. Good atom work with the bad like your right hand an left hand in liftin a boulder. So sayeth Dogg an I guess Johnny Dalton hed agree. Theys iron that curl an iron that stab. Plant Iron Seed to grow new apples. Spill the wine inside the chapels. A yarn for every feather woven in your nest. You always do what you think best.

So Ill tell you the story a Black Wopper. Folk say this an that. Bad storm be a Wopper. Them tree eyes by the Lion I talk about. But folk mostly forget the real Wopper story. Great Mam tell me first. Your daddy she says. He see Black Wopper rise up out the old mill pond right down that road. Rise up like murk an peel a tree an eat it. I dont know why she always want to bring my daddy into it. I didn have no daddy that I knowd of. Ise a foundling. At the sea shore. Ever child should know to be ware the Black Wopper Great Mam says. I knowd a man myself she says. Lose six horses to Black Wopper in right daylight. Garn truth. No good come forgettin it. Well I tell you it she says. Alls you gots to do is listen. Sit down there she says. An we do. It was me an Desmond Carke an Drury McDeane an Lalloway an some others. Youngsters then.

Once a long time gone ago four score fat sheep in Silver Vale there is. Belong to Farmer Bucklethorn. Up Wise Crag an down the other side is Golden Meadow where Farmer Bramble have his fields. Time come to shear sheep. Farmer Bramble ride over Wise Crag an down Silver Vale to help. When theys done with the shearin Farmer Bucklethorn says take this bag a bright wool for your wife. She thank you three times for it says Farmer Bramble. An they settle down for a pipe a backy. Time come to cock hay. Now Farmer Bucklethorn ride up over Wise Crag an down Golden Meadow to help. When theys done at the end a the day Farmer Bramble says take this load a sweet hay for your sheep. They thank you three times for it says Farmer Bucklethorn. An the two settle down for a mug a cider. It go on like so year in year out. Till they beards grow long an they wives grow stout. An they young grow strong an this tales told out.

Cept one fine afternoon Farmer Bramble hes on his way to visit Farmer Bucklethorn. He stop to rest up top Wise Crag an smoke his pipe a spell. Looks back over his land in peace the way a man can do from up afar. Cocked hay down there is like big green stones on a golden field. Farmer Bramble sink into a deep sleep.

Best sleep he ever have in his life but when he wake up he feel a clang in his soul. While he sleep the sky get purple an a chill come on. Well if I go on down he says to hisself Missus Bucklethorn she make her thick potato soup with leeks an celery an fresh butter. I can have me a big bowl an sleep on some a that hay I give em. But on his way the road go dim an a swirly wind come up. Farmer Bramble listen hard. What he hear is a dark low voice like somethin cold hollerin out of a culvert. *Im Black Wopper an Im a gone a follow you. Follow you ever where you go.* Farmer Bramble look over his shoulder an see a big shadow loom across the ground towards him like a black fog boilin up. Then that fog rise up an take the shape of a giant man. Farmer Bramble he hurry on as fast as feet will take him. He dont look back but he hear that terrible voice creep right up over his shoulder. *Im Black Wopper an Im a pick you up an turn you over an shake you bones out a you. You got any coins clinkin in your bumber sack I take them too.*

Farmer Bramble run on an on an down an down till he get to Silver Vale. Help help he cry out. Black

Wopper hes about to turn me over an shake my bones out a me. Farmer an Missus Bucklethorn come run from their house where they was takin supper. You can smell that good potato soup an butter an leeks an dark mossy smoke risin from the chimney. Black Wopper his steam is boilin off a him an he slide across the ground fastern any giant you ever seen. Right up to Farmer Bramble an loudern ever. *Im Black Wopper an Im a shake you over my head an after your bones fall out Im a suck you up an let you rest on the back a my tongue a while before I swallow you down an spit you back up.* Farmer Bucklethorn he come tremblin slow with a pitch fork. You get back an leave him alone he shout. I give you a bag a my best wool. Black Wopper he just wallow back an laugh with his steamy hands folded on his dark smoke hips. *Im Black Wopper. If I want your wool I take me a sheep an shear it with my teeth.* Farmer Bramble bend over red faced tryin to get his breath back. Farmer Bucklethorn says well then I give you two a my best sheep. Take em an leave Farmer Bramble alone. Black Wopper steam an hiss an slub all over hisself gettin bigger all the time. *Im Black Wopper an if I want all your sheep I take all your sheep.* An so he did. That shadow roll slow an thick over the sheep fold an when Black Wopper move off there be not one sheep left. Where my sheep go Farmer Bucklethorn shout. *Ahhhhhhhhh hah hah hah hah.* Black Wopper he laugh his deep mean steamin laugh. Farmer Bramble he begin to get his breath. You give back them sheep he says. Black Wopper boil up big an says *Im Black*

Wopper an my sheep inside me they want some hay. Farmer Bramble he says you give back them sheep I get you plenty a hay. But Black Wopper now he whine out in a high pitch hollow voice. *I never get anything I want.* Just like a giant foggy child.

Well thats all I know. Great Mam she get to this point an then she start coughin an dont stop. Desmond Carke he slap her back an I get some gin berry water dribbled down her but her eyes just sink an she breathe a heavy wheeze. So we lets her lie down to rest. Drury McDeane was tryin to make her go on about Black Wopper so we has to poke him with a stick. We was gettin a bit old for such tales any how. But I always wonder what happen to them farmers. What can you do with a giant fog man. Cant push him off a cliff I guess. Cant poison him neither. Or it may be the key is when Black Wopper he says I never get what I want. What if that be the truth.

Numbered or no your year it start with spring an end with winter. Your day it start with dawn an end with night. Water once flow down from Hog Top dribble to the leaf pond where your bark boats fly forth if they dont get clung up in the rooty shallows. Where they go nobody knows once they get out a your sight. One way only though. Aint no goin back. I ast Pank if he ever hear the end a the tale. The rest aint happen yet he say to me. But Desmond Carke he hear Black Wopper be the soul of a dead man brought back to life by secret machinations. Bolts an gears an chains an pulley belts. Steam engine keep the soul alive. Iron claws for hands. Steam comin out the ears make that fog. Says what he hear is Black Wopper eat up the Bucklethorns and Bramble an all they sheep and hay and then shrink away sobbin an aint been seen again. But he come back Desmond say. You can oath on that.

> *Curse not the king no not in thy thought*
> *Curse not the rich in thine own bed chamber*
> *For a bird in the air shall carry the voice*
> *An that which have wings shall tell all the story*

I reckon I agree with the Black Book on this one. You see that little bird flappin over there. Or it could be a big one I suppose as you dont know how far away he be. Though it seem the little ones is always closer than the big ones. They say some a them birds what fly off in the winter they say some a them birds they fly a thousand miles. Think about a bird flappin flappin flappin all day cross the lonely sky all gray with damp. Just to keep ahead a the vasty winter trailin out behind em. An to keep from fallin. Flappin without stoppin like my heart is beatin. Tryin so hard but dont know what for. Get to the other side a the sky. Wherever that be. I wonder how many miles I walk in all my walkin days. Some one could figure it out with all the multiplyin they do. It may be a thousand but does back an forth add or subtract I wonder. An what about now when I move along on my wheels. Id like to know how far I been but not bad enough to do all that figurin.

Nother kind a figurin is William Doggs so called *Lustrabustions.* Pages he scribble then wad up an thow away while hes mutterin an cursin by the fire while stayin at Maldons. Paper pile up long side the chair with the writin board he rig up wrong side round. Left handed he were. What dont go into the fire any way. Sarah salvage what she can from his drunken revelations an give em to me cause she think it must be like tryin to comb out the message a the birds. An it be worth lookin at his wiggly words from time to time. You see how they change their meanin as your days go by. Look here at this page. Look like hes drawed up a sketch for a place like Withys. Or it could be some kind a castle. This sheet here have some jumbled lines. See there. You cant tell is that a word or a picture. Could be its just his quill spittin ink an dont mean nothin. But you can feel the wrath of it. Them there squiggles with spikes an circles. Could be rods an gears from what they call a diagram. This next bit get tore off when I was slicin a hank a apple bacon on Lalloways back which is like a knotty oak board. She dint mind one bit. She ast me to do it. Slice it on my back Corbel she says. An she bend herself over. Spine bumpin up under her skeezy shirt. Then she start keenin. That weird music like skippin up an down the stair case. I wasnt thinkin that the paper I wrap the bacon in be one a Doggs pages.

But this scribblin you can see through the grease I think may be the roof line a Withys with a little clock there an the top a the sign board. Or if it be words it could be *They fell before the time to link the way.* Or *In fuel we find small fire mans hearts awry.* Though somebody say it haps be Latin. What do you make out down there at the bottom. Next to the circles. Them words there. Ah well. Cant truly tell. It show you that writin it down aint as good as tellin. Writin never seem to satisfy old Dogg any way. Even though that seem to be his main occupation. He says to me one time writins piss frosting on a shit cake. Heres a careful one. You can tell what this is. Shunt bars an cogs an jack wires. Thats a picture a your two man steam fed stockin frame. Pulley wheels up here set amongst the curly clouds. Whole things put on a sky line to make the one machine loom up like a giant buildin. Then that fancy letter C with all them chiseled cornices like on Forty Fours burial plank. Must be Corgabaphel. Thats his bad city. An them tiny runnin figures I think they is down there. They make the stockin frame ten times tall as a man.

Corgabaphel he says. He take up the page hes been workin on. Crumples it. Thows it feebly at the fire an it land on the floor. Not even noticin when Sarah pick it up. Them days was dark visions with black rum. Calandramil be his good city. Some war goin on twixt the two. We all be part of it. Ever thing he say or writes a part of it. I shant be allowed to mortar together this tale of two cities in an edificial manner he says. Nothing but tumbled brick is left to me.

Signs everwhere. Dont have to be a comet or a sick horse aint there. Sometimes the daily thing itself reek with prognostication. Like Dogg tell me about a hump back fellow he seed in one a the Big Town tradin halls where your speculatin jobbers an assorted jack whistlers cant sit down for grabbin notes an promises to pay an flingin paper money through the air. This fine gent make a fortune rentin his hump as a instant desk he run round the floor with for signin contracts on. Hes all French cuffs an powdered wigs. Coats made special to frame his hump with fine trimmins. Ever has the ladies trailin after. No philosopher need to tell you money decide what beauty be. You can see it with machines. Down Big Town they buy up all the so called Fine Illusion lace that Withy can produce. Cog wheel lace we call it. Discard doodle. Fine Illusion. Now thats what you call a ripe old jape.

Doggs up early one morn. Shaved an combed an brushed up like I neer seed him before. Sarah feed an water him. With my other dogs she says. Fitted more or less into some a Bens continental clothes. Ise agreed to company him to his meetin with the magistrate. Bogus matter long forgot he says. A rascal from Corgabaphel has tracked me here. One step along side him an I see he cant walk. Drunk as two masons. Well can you talk I ask him. *The flame from my marrow shall increase their luster* he says. Now thats a proper point a law I says an push him ahead a me down the street. An under his skippy little feet he feel like a hog on ice. Crashin from the kettle yard make him turn to look an he tumble off his pinions flat out in the dirt. Face to the sky. Eyes at peace. Like Silvy smilin afterwards. Hair trailin out in sentimental curls. Aint no use to hale him any farther. Just so sweet a rest is what he need. Not without a bit a mischief though. Cause he aint been easy on Sarah or Ben or me them weeks. Two must be but seem like six. His wernt a face familiar in the square. So Im incline to wonder what may hap if I leave him dropped there in the dirt. I hang my rump over the horse bar an settle down to whittle some pinch pegs. Two hours by Withys clock I watch folk walkin around an even right over him. No one bend a inch to help or find out if hes dead. Like no one see him. Like he dont belong there so he aint there. But Im thinkin William Dogg he be of another element. May be hes angled off somewhere like a stick under water. You give six mice a tincture an three die of it what do it prove. I pump a basin full to splash him awake an first hes pullin on my trou legs an then wipin his face on my crotch an continuin to speak seem just at the point he leave off. Though you cant know for sure. Starving bone boys he says. My fallen magistrate. Calandramils defeated from the outset. Grease the machines. They talk to each other he says. Magistrate. Magister. He an I have words Dogg says. Then he begin to mumble a little sing song.

With a hey and a ho
Sit we down in a row
To pipe a ti do
And drink till we blow
We never say no
So look out below

They say if your feet smell an your nose runs yous up side down. But as he seem to have his feet under him an his head in place I watch him wobble merrily enough down the lane. I like to think he make it to Calandramil one day.

You want to write a story down these days you got to write it down in them countin books. Scrabble your pen cross all them columns an squared off lines if you can find a empty one. Most of em got some numbers on em here an there. Thats all the paper we got now aside from the stacks a big sheets for the steam press what they print the *Notifier* on over to Rumbly Side. Well Ill number off the story for you. One. The birds start talkin. Two. Pank show me the Iron Seed. Three. Silvy go away with her mama I guess. Four. Iron Apples come in. Five. Birds stop talkin. Six. Withys manufactorys built. Seven. Twistin in. Then all the rest of it. Thats what I recall. Though it may be the seed get magnetized before the birds talk. Or the twistin happen while the factory get builded. Or Silvy leave after Iron Apples. No matter though. When things is all pulled along by the thread a fate they can tumble over one another.

So Rose born Croft married old Miller Stonewardens son Burgeon. An Rose Stonewarden when she first get her sack a Iron Seed she says I dont say malice an I dont say menace an I dont say mayhem. But might be another a them M words. Corbel I been markin all a them new sort a strangers roam about. Dont give a hat tip to you. Dont ask for bread or a place to slump a night Rose says to me. Cross your path right in front a you. Put their shoulder in front a your mouth. North south. No direction to em. Times I wish to be movin along myself Rose says. Its my sister Mildred. Gone so far away. An young Rory free a the stocks just long enough to go back in to prison. It age him so she says. Come out he look like Burgeon. Old before his time. Rory he been talkin to some a them folk in prison she says. Four walls an a roof there they say. Out here its what you see. Blankets strung up in the brambles. Coils a thick rope in the middle a the field. Sleep shacks is knobbled up quick out a spaltee lumber leanin which a way she says. Like no one plan to stay but they do. Carts full a beddin. Baskets hangin in the trees. Well Rose talk like this I get a shimmer a my own self livin in my cart as I done back then. I could be one a them wanderers shes talkin of.

Moren once I see a man stalkin the edge a my back fold Rose says. Could be a French spy I suppose like what Ben Maldon an thems talkin about. Though I think Ben he could be one his self. Corbel dont you tell Sarah Maldon what I say. I know youre smart on her. It was just before Sunday last Im over by the spar she says. That good flat rock pointin out over the old meadow. Where they try to make the sun dial that time. I seen the fellow sittin there she says. Well he seen me first. Ise punchin soil to sow Iron Seed you know. Holdin up an shakin the little sack. Right time a the moon she says. Im lookin at it hangin pale up in the day time sky. Big bite out of it sure enough she says. Like eating them little white Izaac Friar apples. I call em moon apples.

> *Apple to apple wit to ween*
> *Iron fat from iron lean*
> *Swell to apple shiny sheen*
> *Iron Seed come to green*

Then I most jump out a my skin Rose says. The feel a his eyes ticklin the back a my neck. Hes as close to me as you right there. Dressed in black. Not movin a near inch. Big eyes float out an pinch me Corbel I declare. He sit right there in my place on that rock. Foreign hat a some kind. Yellow scarf winnowin down his chest. Almost seem like he aint move all mornin long. But I know he wernt there when I brung Rory back his hot bucket.

My nethers turn under an I already got my weak knee pointed his way she says. I cant say how he

get back there thout me seein him. I wernt certain
Corbel if he be a man or a woman. Had your soft
cheeks like Burgeon an hair tied back. Long eye
lashes. No whiskers. But your strong jaw like Rory.
Burgeons mama look like that once. Though its a
time since she been gone. You cant tell what a smile
mean on a face like that she says. Gives you a chill
from behind. Sweet though in a fashion. Aint friendly
nor unfriendly. Like he might vanish she says. I know
about men vanishin in the daytime moonlight. I got
the seed behind my back an I feel like Im holdin a
hot skillet he look at me that way. Im the fool she says
cause sure an dur he seen me chantin on the moon
an all. Oh Corbel apples they come all sour water
now not cider. Im full a worry. This mans cheeks is
the color a the moon. Do he want the Iron Seed or
what from me I wonder. I know them seed be a secret
though no one tell me why she says. So I dont say
a word to him nor he to me. So many new people
comin through put up your guard on all such greetin.
He just tip his hat. Charmin to be sure Rose says.

Tell a true tale if you dont tell nobody she says. Dont
you tell Burge. But theres a man back here one time
not so long ago he get inside me like blue in the sky.
My eyes is fadin now but they be duck green then she
says. Most men look in em an see what they want. Me
I can see truth in the eyes she says. Like you Corbel.
I know them birds confuse you. But you aint tellin no
lies. That day Im takin a bucket a beer to Burgeon

an his boys whos restin in the shade down by the dribble. There be a young one there whos washin out his carolines. He dont see me. The suns dapplin his golden back. Some colors in the trees across the other side I think he must be livin there. Pettihews is chirpin over his head. Dont know what get into me Corbel. But I toss a stick down the bank to make a noise. Just like Ise a rampant little girl. He look up an smile so big on me I almost cry right there. Such a face. Woman know a face like that Corbel. Face to haunt you all life long. Whys Rose tellin me this I wonder. Later I go to him she says. An he give me somethin I remember.

> *They sin who say with lying breath*
> *That love partake of sin an death*
> *Their dead lips the flies draw nigh*
> *Who sin an say that love must die*

What you think of it all Corbel. Well I dint think a nothin I could say to her. Or may be she want to know somethin she dont know how to ask. But since that cheese hut number man who it wouldn make a difference if I killt him an those two what chide me bout the mill pond I been ruminatin on them faces. Somethin is the same about they lookin at me as what Rose describe. Those smiles. Them eyes they underroot your feet while yous standin right before em. They aint ashamed. Stalky neck people lookin down on you. Takin over where you will or wont. Some one pull a string an set em movin. You cant touch em. Dont matter how long you been holdin it they can buy it from the man who give it to you fore you even touch it. Rose say she seen the man again outside the church the followin Sunday. Never take off his hat.

All kind a seed business is in the air. Story from America about special apple seeds. I wonder if thats where the whole thing start. Fellow name Apple Seed John. Walk through the winter with no shoes. Dont wear a hat or coat. Sleeps anywhere. Wanderer like me. Live on salad leafs an hunker nuts an apples an pig berries an cant be happier. He cure ladies from consumptiation an bloody flux with steamin apple presses on their affected parts. He rove into settlements an even talk to red indians. Special books go with him in a sack. He hand em out whenever people tell him they can read. Got three people an only one book he tear the book in three an give it out that way. He say his book is like the loafs an the fishes. Rip it in three an each part have the whole. Even a page contain the whole of it. Even part of a page. Even a single word. Thats what they say. My own thought is this sound like the word inside the word an so it got to be the Green Book William Dogg talk about.

One time Dogg tell about lyin in bed an hearin a whisper that evil spirits want to suffocate him. But he know hes safe on account a his Heavenly Blanket which descend from above. An so he go to sleep. But in the middle a the night he stop breathin an rush up out a his body an see hisself lyin down there on the bed with the Green Book splayed upon his chest. Hes breathin not from his own belly but by a diabolic pump workin on him from above. Dogg recite this in his usual fashion. They attempt to pump my breath out of me but thus far at that they fail he says. Next they try to plant their false black seed in the first chamber of my heart. Theyre admitted to the second chamber when they knock upon the door and wipe their feet. They get their grapples in my vitals. They shoot their igneous lusts into the third chamber. They lave me with their dripping tongues. But I was raised unto a room above he says by hydraulic winches. I made no cry to dispersuade them or a single move to ward them off. That would be a battle which would damage me he says. They got their answer from the doorman of the fourth chamber. Given in black iron words I could not understand he says. Each word blossomed into thousands. It took heavenly efforts for the words to lift the demons. Then there was great peace when they departed. My breath came back into my breast and I came down to join my body under my heavenly blanket once again he says.

But more than just the bag a books John bring his special seeds an seedlins wherever he go. He hand em out an dont want nothin in return. He say thats all right wont you plant em where you can. What people do give him he spend to get more seeds an books. He say the angels in the apple. Apple Seed John's fame spread further than his apples do. This piebald isle a centum worth a seed in a leathern sack we called a penny bag. Though higher prices could be had along the outer roads. A centum come from Apple Seed John hisself once go for two pounds. Easy to get from apple to seed. Hard to get from seed to apple as Izaac Friarll tell you. John Baal. John Apple Seed. Theres two seedsmen for you.

So Iron Seeds is magnetized an steamin under ground. Turnin their direction. Blacksmith strike his anvil but never think about the iron pregnancy that weigh upon the world. Thus Iron Apples. All our ears is pricked up by the mill smashins comin almost ever day now. Macclesfield. Raw Morton. Westhoughton. But what you get aint solid talk. Durin the assizes at Rumbly Side there had been a sentencin. Two men to be hanged. Three to get seven years transport. They was some strong pleadin an mamas tears but no availin. One young chap get two years hard labor down to Munbury mines. One was acquit. All this is from the raid on Maltby an Briggs some months before. Mayor an alderman keep troops on guard there. They must a knowd somethin was about to blow. Could be there was a informer. So the attack wernt so unknown as might a been. Two guard dead I hear an two Ludds men. But such numbers is always chewed on good before theys spat out at you. Cant trust numbers. When it come down to it the only good number is one. Those caught an sentenced were those what get drawd up late in the attack. Forty Four he tell me he see the flames from Maltby an Briggs beatin red up in the cloud all the way out to his place. Next day nine ten times Withy stop in the middle of his steps an look off that direction. Followin night gun powder bombs is blowin up all round. Cant tell where when you hear em but the holes in the ground keep folk stirred up like theys walkin around with socks full a worms. Even Rat Tail Jack lay his wet nose on my thigh to know about it. What can you tell a dog about the ragged ways a man.

Seein poor Will Flowers hanged stir up a lot a folk. He was convicted of shootin a guard in one a the little smashins some while back. But I knowd Will. He never would a done that. Back then things was mostly disorganized so it could a been a accident. An I know he bore a righteous anger at how his father was forced out of his household shop. So I never aks him direct. Such judgment aint for me. But I do visit him in the holdin cell. Aint three steps you can take in there. But them walls talk. Will says ever man ever in there waitin to die was countin his days in blood. Theys seven colors of it that he show me. Seven differnt counts. First is eighteen pointy little strokes angled like sparrow feet on that gray flint. Next to that is twelve fat stripes drippin some at the bottom. Then come a hundred an fifty two on a slant which run right into the corner. I didn count em but Will did. On the side wall you got twenty one thin lines so neat an purple it cant be blood but what else would be in that place an stay to speak like that. Aint pig berry jam. Next to them you got a word that might be *Bear* or *Fear*. Not a number but a word. Thats how some one told their time. How long was it do you think. Then a small faded patch you cant tell how many strokes. Less than a week. That man did not care to live or die Will says. At the far right come Wills own count. Thirty seven when I visit him. Neat an orderly. Bright red. Soon after that come hangin day.

Sheriff Heygates talkin more to the crowd than to Will. You know to take away the life of a man unlawfully is a heinous crime he says. An Will he be the most composed lad I ere did see. The scriptures say so sir he says though I did no such thing. An Heygate says I hope you have made your peace with god an by your repentance you will meet the almighty with a pure soul. An Will he says no one on this wily earth can presume to do that sir. No mortal be pure in his sight. Only our savior go forth from this place into that radiance with a pure spirit. Will turn to the sheriff an say I am quite ready sir. Low but firm. Few can hear it but I be there crouchin under the law table they aint usin for this show. Then the Westhoughton ordinary he look at his pocket clock. It aint a bulby fancy one like Withys. Plain an flat.

After inspectin it for such a time as you think may be it aint workin or he dont know how to read it he mumble out we have ten minutes more. Everbody talk differnt when theys at a proceedin a this nature. Like big bags a sand droop your heart. Im glad I dont have to say nothin. The executioner he turn back the sleeves a Wills green coat which is his brothers from a dress up ball he go to once to meet a duchess. Will press his wrists together an hold em out. So they tie the cords an Will wriggle his hands around an says sir please tighten them, so if I should struggle no trouble will arise. He ask for his sleeves to be rolled down to hide the cords as much as they can. He walk upright as hes conducted through the yard. More alert an self possessin ease at his young age than most a those watchin this awful scene. Sheriffs procession is followed by about two dozen gentlemen a rank. Also a man from the *Notifier*. Theys out to make a lesson of poor Will.

He ascend the scaffold almost with a light step. When he turn he gots I would have to say a cheerful countenance. He ast for nothin but cream bread with strong tea an a dram a tar water that mornin. That have to be part a his lightness. The *Notifier* say later *Competent and calm and even an exulting air.* But what that paper do not say was what Will say. *I did not kill that man.* I hear that soft an clear. What the *Notifier* want is you to think Wills competence an punishment put together they justify justice. But his calm is because he is above it all in his innocence. He look about him from the mount but have no sir no so called exulting air. When the executioner put the sack over his face Will says I would rather it could be done without as I want to see my fate. But Doctor Ford he say it wont be possible. An while the cap is fastened a scattered score or so a folk below is sobbin an shoutin out *God bless you Will. God save you lad* with a choke in their throats. Ise run aroun an climbed the planks behind the scaffold an I hear the ordinary ask Will if he know what the mob is sayin to him. Will says I hear men an women. Not a mob. What do they say. But by that time they aint no more shoutin so the ordinary dont inform Will a the blessins the folk has sended him. Doctor Ford he bend down to pray with Will. Head bent to head about a minute an theys nothin but stiff loud silence all around. Executioner I aint suppose to say but we all know who it is. He go below an make ready to strike out the supports. Big court house clock ring out with a unforgivin tone an while the seventh iron clang is dyin you hear Will an the doctor both prayin with a gulpin fervency. Right up to the point where without no warnin an I swear before the eighth bell sound the supports is knocked away. Will drop out a sight so quick I didn even see it. When I go below he swing knee high above the ground. Doctor Ford hes left alone up on the platform. Unlike most hangins there aint no lewd shouts or rude remarks or pissin drunks or noise a any sort. Only a wee struggle afterward by Will or whats left in his mortal coil. The executioner bein there to pull his heels down hard. Wernt ten minutes after that everone is gone.

Well you listen to me this far. What Im bout to tell you now about our Iron Boy twistin in youre stuck with it. Its yours. Words spoke face to face in the common air you cant undo. Unlike your writ down words which is nothin but a mess a scribbles with many meanins you can thow into a fire. You may go an write this down but I wont sign it. I aint suppose to tell any a this ever. But you wont prove it on me that I did. My only worry is the oath may strike me dead. Me I think the oath itself be dead. We shall see. Ise told of it by Pank. Others by someone else I spect. But no one know whatall about it. Then a parchments posted three four places. No one seen who tack it up. John Gwilt is suckin on his teeth an lookin at it. Tam Brigbys also lookin. Though everbody gots a differnt way a doin that an Tams be sideways. He once work for John back when John was master of a house got ten twelve hand looms. Come a time John move over to the factory when he couldn sell no more. Tam wouldn go with him an dont never get back to regular work. So those two keep some careful steps between em. Many times youd find Tam slumped over in the Lion before noon. Natterin on about the hammers. Hammers this an hammers that. He tap out a rhythm on the table make some folk want to smash a mug on his fingers. Hammers wake you now he says. That pilchin fuckin twankin. Damn mill hammers wormin in your sleep. Disturb your waken. Metal chinkin fuckin goblin racket. Devils grindin day dont never stop he says. Tam keep his teeth together like that when he talk you can tell the rum is bangin him bad. Where be the axe a my forest father. Where be the solid chark a gods good wood he says. He slam down his fist. One morn it be right on you. Then the next the next the next you wake up there it is he says. Keep on just enough to make ya shout a missus. What dang things this nonsense May he says. She dont say nothin. Damn wife dont hear squatty grunt a what you say. Them hammers hit you up inside he says. You feel em in your bones. Behind your eyes. Dont say you dont he says but he aint talkin to anyone. Sure as fuck aint nothin for it in this place. He slap his glass on the table an wobble out the door. Thats Tam before the twistins.

So there everbody is a lookin at these tacked up sheets.

> *You might as well be hung for death*
> *As breaking a machine*
> *So now your trusty sword unsheath*
> *And hone it sharp and clean*
> *Be ready men the cause to join*
> *Whenever we may call*
> *Make foul blood run clear and fine*
> *Of tyrants great and small*

Thats chill enough to read in the mornin air. The line

a bloods not yet been drawn but now our finger tips is gettin dipped. Explosions in the night. Flames in the clouds. Transport to kangaroo land. Talk a more hangins an worse. Rumors of a new French blade brought in by night. Tall chopper in a frame they lock your bare neck into. Next you see the head a some one you know a rollin down the street. Just the thought of it thicken your throat. There was some smaller writin down below.

> *Remove this who dare*
> *They shall sup on tyrants fare*
> *For King Ludd is everywhere*
> *And he can see and hear*
> *Half way back*
> *From the monkeys crack*
> *First tree on the left*
> *Sherwood Forest*
> *Or what remains of it*
> *Signed in blood*
> *By King Ludd*

Thats all they was. Smudgy patch at the bottom could be blood if you want to think it so. John Gwilt an Tam Brigbys not lookin at each other but they know they gots to talk. I see Lalloway larkin next to the factory waste pile. Sarah Maldon got a tremble on her eye an a sad pinch on her lip corner. Her Bens away in France as usual. Desmond Carke pole faced as ever. I did not see Pank. Sarah she go an take to her bed. Might a been the first sign a the affliction what would later confine her though we couldn know that yet. I bring her over a kettle a turnip soup but she just let it sit there in the cold dark till the fat crust it over.

Theres a good bit a buckin an blowin off that day. Couple a mill fights. Word go round theres four horses was stole in Dutch Town. They say six sheep was leadin a man an a dog round a fairy loop over to Raw Morton. Later they find a strangled lass from Child Town on the bleachin field by the river though that may not a been connected. What I didn know is our twistin in be that very night. Bout the time the moon rise behind the Knob theys a knock come on my cart door. I crack it open. See a tall lady cloaked up in a mans long coat. Moon shinin behind her head. Then I make out the scarf an rouge blossoms on the white powder cheeks an a collar ruffle under the wig. Pank who look somewhat like a lady in a play. He give me the sign like this. I dont know how far wes goin so I grab me a handful a pig berries from my stash an follow him over the bleachin field. Turns out I forget about them berries an some days on theys a stinkin mush in my side sack I stick my hand into. We aim up the path towards Gilly Vale then we jig west. Climb over the stone fence to make for Colmehin Hall. Full moon that night. Must a planned it so. You can feel it grabbin on you. Some you can an some you cant but this moon pull strong on your insides as it rise up the sky. I feel like a ghost walkin two inches off the ground. It did make everthing look mooly an not like itself. Later I says to Pank you know bright moon light aint the way to hide your doins. Why not twist in at the new. He just plod on ahead like Grim Slim.

Colmehin Halld stood empty longs I can remember. Wernt a proper hall so calld but a eight sided structure sit way back along the old cinder track. The lady a Colmehin die a young widow. A gingerbread hawker tell me its from a hex set by a old witch named Rumnilla an her daughter Nellivora on the Dutch folk who once live down that road. They was burnt an the ashes stirred in pitch an lye an buried an then the long wadin pool was put in over em by that baron who died there after. An its true them trees along the cinder track is twisted skeletons clawed up black from burnin or disease an you can feel somethin hangin in the air. One winter I crunch along under them grabbin branches an it feel like the world shrink to an arms length an iron winter be frozen over you like a dark bell. Its true the Dutch folk what once live along that road did all die out an their houses rot an sink into the mire except for some riddled shingles an splintery spars an rusty continental nails. Though that stuffs all long gone. Some of it to build the Child Town huts. You never hear it called Dutch Town till them Dutch is dead. Now Colmehin Halls the only thing standin thereabouts. Someone must a tended it all those years. Eight sided so you dont know front from back at first through the night. It look dim an grand across the field under that brass moon which is shrunk from havin rose up in the sky while we was walkin all that way. But gettin closer I see why *gloom* come out a *loom.* Children they dont never play up there. I never did. So I follow this man woman Pank. Skys started glowerin a bit. Big rips a cloud movin fast up there. That dabby moon shootin in an out. I get a cold jump in my gut when a branch on a bush move in at me like I owe it somethin. Then I see eight nine others followin likewise their own leaders in little groups up to the door from differnt directions. We come to the column portico that wrap around the whole structure. Eight tall arches full a little pane windows. Dark because theys curtained up tight inside but also smeared with years a dirt.

Must a been bout fifteen twenty of us new ones millin in the door way. Plus eight ten or so a those what bring us there. I go in an a man like a butler give me a dirty pink mask with a pig snout an pointy little ears. I says to him my face be my own mask but he dont like the joke I guess. Others already got a mask or costume or is smeared up in lamp black or stage paint with a wig. First thing inside that place is a wide hallway run round the whole eight sides. Candle lamps in front a mirrors everwhere. If you aint seen nothin like you has to be impressed. You expect some jokin but there aint none a that. Floors shined up gleamy as Withys pay table. Butler man says take your shoes an boots off. Ever one look wide eyed. Shufflin in our stockins like a new calf in the kitchen. I see a lady in pants an leathers an a man in a baggy flowered frock. Later I wonder why they never talk about Iron Girls. Some I know who they is right off but theys good disguises all in all. Pank hisself in fancy crinoline an padded out to fill the bosom. You almost think its in a provokin way. Black curly wig from a operetta. Stage powder an a beauty mark on his cheek. He have a coquette mask he hold up to his eyes with a handle. Smart handsome lady that Miss House. You might run behind her sloppin your mug to find out more. A maskll fool you. With the muscles workin in the jaw an that ridge on his nose an a bit a stubble Pank might be a cacklin witch. You know who he is yet your eye want to tell you somethin differnt. Desmond Carke hes costumed up like his own self. Leather apron. Thick blousy shirt to keep the sparks off. Face smeared with ash. I never hear him say nothin yea or nay about machines or smashin. He just pang his anvils for the factory repairs. Well that boy he do keep his stove lids sealed. It were a night a big surprises. And greasy Lalloway. Why shes in this I dont know. Better to let her than have her squawkin. Shes wigglin in black breeches an a mans ruffled shirt. Long hair hid under a round tub hat. No mask but her face is smudged up here an there though not much moren usual. Then I note it aint her usual dirt at all but more careful painted on dirt. Since she dont take much care she strut about like this for two weeks after. Pank worry but I tell him no one pay any mind to Lallo. Why would you.

Lallos dartin eyes is watchin everbody but she got her way to make it seem like only you. Well wes all knowin about her I do hope. Did get some kind a rise out a me her dressed up like a man like that. John Gwilt he was brung in last of all. There wernt much time to worry. They herd us round the hallway to the other side. Its slippery to pad your way on that bright floor so everones careful.

Fat drapes with tassels is hung over the door way to the inner sanctum. Its a eight sided room with a big gold dome up top. Hung with thick blue curtains all around the walls. Bout twice as big as the back room at the Green Lion but five times as tall I guess. Goin round above theys an open inside walk way lined with books an grimy portraits you cant make out. Tall tall tapers in tall greek sticks is set measurely round the sanctum walls. Flames is straight an narrow an them deep blue curtains hold back a luster like a kingly coffin lining. I wonder bout that so called Lady Colmehin. Dont see how anyone can do much livin in such a place. Although you might point out I live in a cart so who am I to ask that kind a question. Now they range us round the room. Mistress Pank open a door that lead to a hidden stair case an I see Colmehin Halls a craftier place than first appear. Out come a person all in black an a big painted mask helmet what go over his or her whole head. Remind me a the time we painted a face on a bucket an put it on New Billys head an then beat it with spoons. Well

I was younger then. We all was. Im sure you note how many folk is dressed in black in this here tale. Tell me if you got a idea what it mean. I do. But Id like to hear yours first.

Then a hollow voice come from deep beyond itself. *Once only shall you see me and only in this semblance and no otherwise. But you shall not forget.* Things get deep real quick now an theys some coughin an stiffenin an clearin a the throat all round the ring. Is this church or what you can tell some is thinkin who dont go there much. *For as the seed comes out of the dark earth our oath emerges from this very night. Come the light of day our oath will be said and done and yet not done. But its fruit you shall not eat. Only the seed survives to enter the dark earth again. And so the generations beget the generations. From this our joining place two paths go forth side by side. Like unto the tracks of a cart one wheel of iron and one wheel of mahogany. But the cart shall one day come asunder. The two wheels shall diverge. The tracks shall part and go their separate ways. Thus do the two poles of the magnet bend the Iron Seed in two directions.* Then the voice go silent. Everthing is froze in place. Even the candle flames is like on ice. That eight sided room rise up like music with no notes except I feel a little tremble. I cant tell if its my knees is shakin or what as I dont look down. Now come the oath. Thats the word must strike iron terror in the land those days as it figure in all the harshest punishments. So called oathin they fear more than the smashin. Cause they can break a frame breaker but a oath dont break.

The master a these revelations goes round the circle like the hands a Withys factory clock an near as slow. Puttin candles out one by one with a three foot snuffer an holdin a gleamin gold sword straight up with the other hand. An every time a flame snuffs out theres a low bell like from a far off cathedral cept there aint nothin like that round there. Flame by flame the room grow dark in dyin shades a blue. Gleam fade out inch by inch across the shiny floor. My hearts beatin in my ears. Just before it go all dim I catch Lalloways flirty eyes which are always there whenever you look up. Why she always got to be straight across from me I wonder. Her dirty grin just then be disturbin to the occasion an I fear what she may bust out with. I can just about hear one a her silly songs bouncin in my head.

> *Christmas Eve I turn the spit*
> *Burn my thumb and feel it yet*
> *Sparrow cock jump on the table*
> *Pot begin to beat the ladle*

You know the one. It go fastern faster with Lalloway runnin round you an hittin at you with a switch. Another time she come up to you quiet with a little book. Look at my new almanac she says. She do have a sweet voice when she try. Then she snap it on your nose with her smile.

Then the oath take charge. *This our Iron Seed shall gird the nations of the earth for the darkness still to come upon us. One day it shall bloom in all the lands and multiply as all the stars of heaven. Repeat now after me. Line by line and doom by doom.*

> *With this sacred oath*
> *I weave my word and will*
> *With those of every Iron Boy*
> *Our mission to fulfill*
> *These very words are one*
> *An oath to set us free*
> *And never shall it be undone*
> *Unto eternity*

So that be the iron oath. Dont sound like so much do it. Well things is changed since then. Was a time when wernt a man had ever seen corn sowed by steam drill or thrashed by devil rotors. A eight year old could fill pillows one by one from the pickin bag without havin to stuff em quick as theys movin by on a pulley belt. None the less you may want to prick your finger now an suck your blood while you count to ten.

Well I guess I aint died from tellin you this. So if theys danger now its yours not mine. What you do with its none a my concern. So we say the oath an now there come a harp in the dark. Little bells chime in an a tambour tappin an a fiddle scrapin announce the dance. Cant have a floor like that without some dancin on it. I once went over to the grand dance pavilion in Dangington but couldn get my feet to move. That floor was shinier than this one. Ladys dresses an faces an bright lights was all doubled an I couldn look up from it. I wernt no good at dancin even when Nancy try her game with me. Moving both feet at once on a slick floor I just fall over or bobble round like a skittle. I find me some other ways to make a lady smile. But not dancin be a disadvantage sure an dur.

One time Tam Brigby an Forty Four an Desmond Carke pile leg a belly up top the ice wagon. Ride over to Spindleford for hangin day. We was just lads then so this is long before the Luddish hangins. These hangins is for your usual kind a monkey business. Pony thievin an wrongful writin an simple murder an such. I wouldn go with em. Nothin to do with it. Next day they come back snarkin up their sleeves. Curlin fingers round the others necks who snap down limp like a shot duck. I dint like their gleamin eyes. Bad boys some ways they was. Always pushin a stick up the rear end to see what poop out. It was Desmond tweak me on it. Says Corbel dont you want to dance the Cutty Mun. We seen it over to Spindleford. Give up Corby he says. Ever man can dance the Cutty Mun. We teach you how. Tam kick my heels an Desmond grab my neck from behind so Im hangin there. I tell em to go piss rope. An Desmond he says rope. Thats it Corby. Cutty Mun the dance a man do on the end of a rope. Ever man dance good to that tune he says. Cream yourself with the pleasure of it Corby he says. He flail his skinny self around tryin to choke me but I thow him off. Damp pants on you not me I says. There be many kinds a dance to haunt you.

When we light them candles back up one by one with a golden torch passed hand to hand the room seem bigger than before. Next to the door by the hidden stair case sits the harp lady an the tambour man all dressed up like an Elftown Ball. Oath master aint no longer there. Music jumps up an we get moved into a tight little square. Theyll always be those who know what to do. Rest of us just muddle along till we be drug in to the pattern.

Pank grab my hand an pull me over. How do these folk get to be in charge a us Im thinkin as I look at him up close now. An the likes a Desmond Carke bein with us. Youd never suppose hed be a part a such a thing. Make me think I aint been watchin out sharp. Them birds distract me. So now I just hie one foot in front a the other an stumble along behind. Didn want to be the first one twisted but I was thick up in it now. I count sixteen folk make up the outer square. Nine a us new twisters in the square inside the square. So one by one they take us up an spin us out an spin us back down through the lines. One through nine I guess. Im tryin to remember Nancys little dance but this ones got more to it. Back an forth an back an forth an everbody turnin like gears in a clock works you might say. First row I believe it was old Bairn grab me by the crotch an collar an spin me like he dont want no mistake about it. Im rollin off his belly an about to kiss the next ladys beard. Roll me bum round into the row beyond an here come Lalloway fore I can get my self prepared. I cant dance but I can shuffle good so I jerk my shoulders round on her to keep from lookin in her eye. But I feel her floppy dugs wormin at my back an her breath close up on my neck an was it her who whisper my name like a question. But I dont got time to wonder since Im glad to get around to some nice lady I dont know an then John Gwilt in the last row. By then I been felt over like a Dutch piglet. Its a bouncy grindin machine. Not the kind a dance I ever seed before. Up an back an up an back an spittin us out the other side one by one. An the music. I dont know what to say. Like nothin I ever heared before. Like someone took a tune you know an twisted it backwards. Like that. Now Im through the mill I can watch the others till it be my time again. Its Sarah Maldon next. Got a mask an Bens old buck skins on. How was it I didn see her there before or know when I was rollin against her. I wonder did she give a sign to me through the fray an did I miss it in my fluster. But you cant ask about things like that. Folk dont even know what they do in such strange occasions. At the end its Mistress Panks the one give me the final twist. He kiss me on the forehead as he slap my rump an flounce against my leg. Then he bring his gloved fist down right sharp upon my head.

Thus crowned Im breathin hard an musked up in my agitation. This men an ladies dressed like the other aint a thing I got a firm grasp on. But now we was all twisted in. Then we get our numbers. Some do any road. As it turn out only the fellows. Ladies dont get em. Dont know why that is. An if you ask you wont find out. Iron Boys an the twistin its the only thing I believe in for a time. Even birds I listen to em good but never do believe like true believe. May hap theyll forgive me. I still listen to em. But I cant believe em any more.

Aint nothin left a the twistins now. Everthings forgot. Cept Forty Four I guess. He dont forget. An yet he dont remember neither. But that night the moons declinin when we come out all roused like golden spangle dust has drifted down an burnished our cheeks. We take off our masks an everone look round at the others smilin silent. Then we march off on our separate ways to home. Now we aint led but now we aint alone. Twisted in. An whats twined between us wont be spoke of in the light a day.

> *Boldness this night we have sung.*
> *Now have we ears instead of tongue.*

After that pig line race at Fool Fair they was stakes an cords strung out all across the field for months seem like. More land strung up than seem required. Theys slicin up the fields back then like no tomorrow. You read it in the *Notifier* ever week. *An Act for Inclosing*

Lands. Notice hereby bein given. Commissioners appointed by parliament. In whatever year of the reign a his present leech head majesty. At a meetin held by adjournment they did set out an conjure an privately determine the carriage roads an donkey ways an foot paths that is set through lands an grounds to be inclosed for a manufactory an its out buildings an storage yards an egresses an what not. What are you gonna do.

Like this. One carting road. Begin at the southeast corner of a garden belong to Jonathan Wrench an his wife Elizabeth. Proceed from there in a west direction an near in a straight line across the pasture belong to the square once called Town Common. To the southeast corner of a previous inclosure a land called Jockey Pightle belong to Thrushton Mort Esquire. An from thence nearly in the same direction an nearly in a straight line to the middle dole a said Thrushton Mort. To the southwest corner where it enter the parish a High Stocking which road is called Gravel Cross. Thence to join the Southing road which pass by the west side of the said manufactory plot. An like this. One donkey way. Begin east end a last described carting road. Proceed from thence in the northeast an east directions to the southwest corner of a previous inclosure of land called Biffs Bottom belong to Robert Pule occupation of robin hopper. Thence to north side of the said manufactory plot. Like this. One private foot path. Branch out a the earlier described donkey way at the northeast corner of the disputed inclosed two acre patch called Cockfester Close belong to Reverend Theophilus Girdlestone author of *The Arithmetic of Real Life and Practical Business, to wit: The New Improved Grammar of Commerce Trade and Manufactures.* But disputed by owners of the adjacency to the Sir Isaac Newton a public house some ways in a line east from the proposed entrance to the said manufactory. Thats about the size of it. Thats how they publicate their intentions but the plans is all foredrawn. The diggers an the carts an stacks a bricks an boards an sacks an black rod pipe an pulley wheels an such already brung in aint no surprise though some pretend it be. An shit aint none a that language in the *Notifier* sound a whit like the roads an paths an donkey ways you an I walk on. Those folk aint even the real owners. But the *Notifier* do chart everwhere it is my feet use to go an couldn go now if I still had em.

Everone stop five six times a day to watch Withys manufactory goin up. Just as fascinatin as a fire takin down a buildin. But slower. They have to start chasin people away whos so intent they aint doin they own work. Them travelin masons an joisters make rude jests an shout an spit an drop bricks on local folk from up on the stilt platforms. But too soon that buildin stand there firm an dont look like to go away. It block out the part a the sky where the moon use to set. Wernt a square here before. Just that field where the pig race be. An much a the Fool Fair. They top the buildin off with a pine tree got a pig skull strapped to the tip. That supposed to tell god we aint goin any further in your sky. Its a lie a course. They could if they would. Weeks a scurryin an clatterin within. Clangin an cursin. Explosions like you wonder if they know what theys got bottled up in there. Goodly thing they chase folk away. Steam bolts fly out gapin window holes. Twice a day an more you hear a fat black pressure bang. One a them bolts hit the lantern in front a the County House an whats the odds on that. Crack in the glass still there. Then the regular clankin you can hear clear to Six Acres start up when they connect the boiler pistons to the shafts an belts. Delicate business they claim even though your shanks an cogs is made a iron. You must assume some folk gets pleasure from machines. No one look at Withy an think elseways. He appreciate all the hard pumpin pleasures of machinery. Shafts greased an slidin in an out the collars. Got to remind you a somethin. One time before Silvy Ise with a frosty dame in Golspie who did an didn want to. I plugged her hard an regular just like that but couldn get my seed grabbed right. Couldn spring her loose by poundin nor me neither no matter how long I keep at it. Finally I just fall down on top a her an we lay there worse than before.

Withy hes there to watch all big eyed. New parts arrive an he aint curbed by modesty. Planetary axle is wrapped up with the fly wheel under big thick folds a chudder cloth. Withy slip his tremblin smilin hands around like you caress a ladys hip bones under her petty coat. Run his fingers up an down the greasy shaft until he hit that soft hard leather valve what squeeze the piston joint to keep the pressure up. Then he fling off them chudder sheets an his oily engine parts lay shinin fair before him. I swear he about drool. His face be all blotched an hes heavin breaths with wheezy fervor. Them steam tight glands aint yet pinioned on the collar a the stuffin box. So as they turn the wheel the large piston dont meet its socket but wave about stiff in the air in blind punches. Poke ever which way above an below that greased crupper. The engine men is growin impatient with Withys agitated hands on everthing though they cant say no a course. At last they get him out the way an eight men guide the shaft into the hole which is still so stiff an new it wouldn take it in at first despite the sweatin efforts of all them hefty fellows.

Foreman he finally get the giant waggin head a that piston shaft engaged at the same time the men is thrustin. So the change a angle sink it hard home all a sudden to rotation depth in the leather gland with a soft sighin slide. Foreman shouts *Hot puddin for supper* an theys big shouts all round. Withy hes so worked up he fall back on his bum with the final thrust. He dont see the rollin eyeballs of his engine handlers. Hes just pantin an clingin to the rack beside the beam.

Ise thinkin a the story bout how Withy first derive his business methods. Young George age a ten is sharp as tacks when his mother die. Hes taken up to Dangington to work in his fathers mill. A tiny pearl belong to his mama is given to him for a keep sake. He stash it in the pocket of his jerkin so he always have it with him. One day young George he come upon a raw John Clod whos wanderin down the high way with a ragged eared donkey. George offer to make a instant trade thereon. Pearl for donkey an donkey for pearl. John Clod he says but I need my donkey for tonight. Young George says you keep this pearl then. It remind you to meet me here tomorrow an conclude our bargain. That slant head Clod with his hair stickin out arrive next morgen at the same spot with the donkey lyin dead on a cart. Says bad hap. Donkey get boulder gut an swell up in the night an now look at him. George says Ill have back my pearl then. Clod says well no. I give it to the landlord on a debt. George says then I take my donkey. John Clod says what for hes dead. George says I put him up to raffle. Clod says how do you raffle a dead donkey. George tell him you go hoe your own row. An he drag that stinkin donkey off. Month or so later John Clod an George meet up again. Clod says what happen with your donkey. George says well I put up a sign. *Donkey tickets one penny each.* Sold five hunnert. Course the man who won the dead donkey want his penny back George says. I just give your land lord three hunnert for my pearl. So you see Im plus a hunnert ninety nine he says. Im happy. Your land lord is happy. An I dont know what you are John Clod but thank you sir. Withy leave Clod in the middle a the road scratchin his stick out hair.

UNDER THE WALL

Under the wall corner closest to the Court House is the same spot where there was a fellow buried durin the buildin. Some says its the ancient code. You has to kill someone to undergird the startin stone. For example Ophiuchus lay the foundation stone a his pearly gate house upon the femur of his first born son. Thats well known. An they say the main gate a Big Town was orientated accordin to a silver needle floated in a alabaster bowl tremblin to the lip with virgins blood. An that virgin she was laid there under Ludd Gate in a gold coffin. Its Nimrods decree. There must be stuff an substance down under of enough weight an circumstance to counter what you build above. An a man or a virgin it gots a lot a that kind a weight. Nimrod the mighty warrior. His kingdom was the land a Babble. He slew an buried ten thousand eight hundred an forty four souls in one big pit to shore up his mighty spire. But his ambition oertopped the lot. Look what happen to his Babble Tower. Pieces of it fallen everwhere an carted off. May even be some here they say. Come foundation day Withys there to tamp the footstone with the trowel handle an say whatever you say on such occasions. An this young feisty mason dont know where hes from they call him Bob got the stone set there in glistnin mortar with the graven side to eastward. Right behind hims the open pit from when it was dug for Demonstration Day. Thats the day when Withy announce the exhibition of what he call *The Raising of Water by the Impellant Force of Fire.* First trial a his steam engines an he want to calculate what they can do. How much so called horse power.

What it come down to is they has to figure a way to say what a steam engine can do that a man can understand. You raise this much water that many feet with this much steam you calculate how many horses it take to do the same. So they dig the pit an some gents from Mechanick Arts set twelve dray horses to compete against a engine pumpin water from the bottom a the shaft. They say them horses pull up if I get this right they pull twenty two thousand pound a water out a the pit on the chain winch in ten minutes. Thats what they say but I say no horses can do that. What them tough old horses do I hear is they raise twenty two hundred pound in one minute. Them horses is strainin an foamin at it an one of em give out. Slide down off his legs an get drug back tangled up side down in the wires holdin the pit winch. Killt him quick. No way them horses can work like that all day. But the man doin the measurin he overdrive em to get his numbers where he want em. But even when he divide out that poor dead horse it aint enough for him. He add eleven hundred to get what he call machine horse power. Aint twenty two no more but thirty three. Thirty three hundred pound in one minute. Add back the naught an you get your thirty three thousand. Why. You ask me aint nothin but a way to make them numbers bigger. It aint what your honest horse fleshll do under the sun. Why even call it horse power. If its a horse its a horse. Power be somethin else. I never make Gladden pull if she dont want to. Id rather walk or stay put. Mostly she want to though. But it just be my cart. So what was all them horses pains an drivin em to death around a axle for. Horse power mean the devils out dancin an he aint never stoppin. They say your engine is like a heartbeat only stronger. Cause it dont get sad or give out all together. But even when my heart beat faster like when I run after Nancy it dont feel like that. Cause your heart it aint just one poundin an rotatin thing. You feel it in your head an your neck an your stomach an your knees. When youre awake in the night nowdays an you hear that *skreak skreak skreak skreak skreak* across the dark an you think it sound like a night wiper or a tit pincher you know it aint. Not one a them birdsll say the same thing five times exact like that without a modulation. You know it be the squeakin a machines. An if theys imitatin birds or birds is imitatin them well I leave that to you an your man Friday.

So no one know this young travelin mason more than to call him Trash instead a Bob for pourin his soup can down on New Billy one day just to get a laugh. He hand the little golden hammer to Withy an point his pointer where to tap the stone in place. Suns in everones eyes an Pank tells me next thing is this fellow Bob fall backwards in the pit an the foot stone tip back after him an crush his head down there. Fall or pushed no one seem to say but whatever happen that pits filled up so quick its poor Bobs grave an hes forgot before you start to remember him. Bob an the birth a so called horse power is buried right there under that wall corner. I may be the only one recollect it now when everthings forgot. Where theres fire there will be smoke Pank says. After the Bob business he set out on the road. Nine month later he come back with the Iron Seed an magnetizers an thats where we begin. Factorys runnin strong an smokin up the sky by then. Only four floors but like the Babble Tower it got stairs go nowhere. Doorways sealed over. Inside passages of a dubious servitude. Staircase run up round a corner an into a blank wall. You do find strange beauties in a factory though. New lights an shadows. Things come to look clearer in its light an motions. You hear the tiny clickin a the grace spikes finishin off the cloth and you think theys polishin up the very air.

One dark autumn night the wind blow rain sidewise through the copse. South side a Withys. Yellow shower a little round leafs like gold coins on the wet path in front a your boot toes. An you wouldn a seed em that way an they wouldn a made you smile cept in the new light pourin from the factory windows. Machines is tryin to spin gold too fast to see. Me I put my loot in a sack and dont say where. But the way now is your manufactory got twenty five thousand motions big an little belted to the steam shaft. Twenty five thousand two hunnerd and fifty three. Each motion makin money. Only way they know the number is Withy hire some men to count em. What use now be your very own fingers. Wigglin this way an that way as you pluck a stitch or smooth down the fluff or pinch the tuck or lay over the cross bar or stuff a pillow bag. You look down the long preparation room. Flakes a cotton fly out a the cardin jaws light as snow. The rest is seized by the spinnin teeth an stretched out into skeins a spider thread too quick to see. Little spools flow like mad tricks into the whirlpool. Big spindles whiskin round above your head. Shuttle shoot across an back across an back untouchin. What it do is like to scratch a never endin itch. Somehow all the speed make me think death be always hoverin an he come quick in there.

Embroidery though is what can most transfix you. Sprigs an flowers. Hearts an doodads. Leafs an windin stems an honey combs an hop clusters. You name it you can see it dart forth from the self impulsion a the needles. So fast you try an mark out a single stitch an you cant. The whole appear to grow there like a pretty little stain spreadin before your eye. An your eye feel slow. Or you blinked or somethin.

Enchantment a some kind is takin place. It be bright but somehow sad when you watch them needles go. Things go faster yet you gots no time to figure it. *Works is larger than the man.* Thats what Withys always sayin. Why he want that to be so I wonder. Even tiny things is larger than the man now. Faster. *Not this valley but the world.*

I could never stack it. I try workin them stockin frames a week or two but it aint healthy. Thats after poor Gladden she go off to the knackers yard. Later on I bang down my old cart to sticks an make a chicken house for Sarah. But in them two weeks heres exactly what I learnt to do. Thow the thread from the bobbins over the hooks. Draw the slur down by the treadle. Force down the jacks an sinkers. That get your loops tween ever pair a needles. Then you sink the sinkers. Lock up the jacks by thumb to equalize the loops. Thow up the frame spring. Push down the presser bar by foot. Hang the web you made on the needle brads there in the groove. Bring down the frame to the bottom standard. Catch the work on the sinker webs. Theys the ones look like long little archies there. Next you let your frame rise up to the coping catcher pressin on the thumb plate. Then you move one course to the right an start again. I learnt all that. Do it without stoppin so the yardage flow like water. An I wont forget it to my dyin day. Aint that a shame. Cause I dont need to remember. Machines do the rememberin. Even the feet I dont got any more they still know what to do on the treadles. But to tell it sound like much moren it is. You hardly move in your spot. Thing is you gots to do it quick. Hundred yard an hour the sisters is suppose to fold. Enough to make you tired when you wake up in the mornin. But it wernt the work or motions get me. Twas some other grindin thing about it. All them whinin machines belted up in tow. I come out in the air after what they call a shift an I feel like Im tapped all over. Way you dimple down the metal on a shield. Like Brigbys pilchin clankin hammers hes on about. My joints is achin an I feel like the start of a puddlin croup under my ribs. Heart jumpin little hedges for no reason. Thats me. But those as tolerate it feel right fine. More chance to pinch the ladies an nuzzle em under all the noise in there. They never be short a workers. Folk stream in from ever direction.

Theys always a bad corner to a place. One you cant squeeze out no matter how you shift the stuff around. It be that place you cant fit things or they get lost or dont work right or catch a fire. Some folk say you best call that a cursed spot an be done. Else its just where a train a bad events piles up all its jingle jangle. Bad corner a Withys is Bobs corner. Ground floor right above his burial place. Just across from the shaft room which lead up to the clock works. First they put the hankin jenny there. Had to move it out when the hanks come off the spindles ever time you turn around. Then they put in the battin bench but it keep shakin itself out a place ever time they shim it against the wall. Next Withy set paymasters desk there an hang a lantern above it. Lantern aint up two days fore it come down crashin an burn up half the count book. Smoke up the pay masters wig as well which is lyin there for some reason. Cant find nothin else. Cardin engine its too long. They try an move the center post to make more room but the whole floor above sag like to tumble. Another bit a trouble or two like that they call it a bad spot an leave it empty. Though accordin to William Dogg they aint no such a thing as empty. Always somethinll fill that space whether you see it or no. Devils fill it if no other thing be fit. Be like that also with that shiny silkeen cloth Withy invent. Bad pucker spots in it you can try an smooth out by shovin em around or pressin on em. Squeeze em a little here a little there. You need to keep your shuttle screwed down tight all across the bar to get the smoothness in silkeen. You get your suckin puckers if the threads is all aligned with the same curve in the backs. Suck your whole line out a warp you can lose a day an a half. I wonder if thats like magnetizin. Take silkeen off the rack an you can push them puckers round from one spot to another. Blend em in to one big pucker like a sheet a that India rubber. But with silkeen the whole dang thingll never lay down flat if it dont at first. Specially with your fancy ladies clothin you dont want them puckers goin the wrong way round a ladys curves.

Do you ever think a the word *machine*. *Machinery*. Or on the other hand *mechanical*. Machine it got a soft sound could be like some kind a old French cloth. Mechanical you hear the claw an ratchet in it. Machine I think more dangers in the word on that account. Mechanical you hear it clear enough. I wont speak a machinations. But I seen the big ratchet claw in Withys clock works run away with itself one time sure an dur. Back when his big sign was still new. Or not new but the hole had just been cut inside the big *C* in *Co* for the clock dial to go in to. Them roman numbers get pressed all round the rim. Splayed out upside down an sideways like it dont matter what you think. An what about the night time any way. Same numbers as the day. Black hole in the middle an no so called hands spanged onto it yet. They call it a face though I fail to see why. You know them folk says they got no use for a clock. Thems the very first ones walkin the square awaitin the arrival of it. Clock hands was brought in on a special wagon from Baggerborough. Not from the clock factory there but from some other firm do fancy brass cut work. All the use I can see in that clock lookin down on us is therell soon be gangs at Withys doorway as the stockin girls an mill boys queue up waitin for the bell to work the shifts. An soon enough the fines is posted everwhere.

> *Any come ten minutes after the bell – two shilling*
> *Any refuse to work after the bell – two shilling*
> *Any putting his gas out too soon – one shilling*

> *Any relieving hisself more than twice a day — six pence*
> *Any being sick cant find another — six pence*
> *Any washing his self before noon — one shilling*
> *Any shaving over ratchets or spikes — six pence*

It be like that an folk dont say a word. Just do as theys told. You burp an fart at the same time they fine you.

> *Any counting his hours before pay master — one shilling*
> *Any wave out the window at anything or nothing — six pence*

Who can remember em all. An they dont enforce em except when they do so who knows. But ever one was gay impatient to see that clock start up. Maggie Moats think now she get Barley home sooner. Though I know old Barley Moats. He gonna see things crooked from wherever he sit. Maggie say seven he say eleven. In his mind he gonna bend them brass hands like tin flanges. An your popish numbers dont help none. As it is Barleyll puff his self up pointin at the dial an crow out *Ix. Ix. Vi. Vi. Bend your knee an elbow to the new Sumerian gods*. Aint no clock handll point that man home sooner or soberer. Old Barley he only shave his self about the lip so he dont waste no dribbles from the bottle.

So when them hands come in on a long wagon hitched behind the mail coach Withy stand over while his boys pry the lids off the crates. Theys shined to gleamin an almost delicate in tracery despite the size. Big enough to say whichever way they point its the right way. Curls an fleurs cut in em like kings mischief. More like arms than hands is what I think. Little one I could just about stretch arm pit to finger tip. Big one might be a foot longer. Or fancy dubbin swords they could be. For the Christmas play. More like that than hands any road. So Withy need some help that day to collar an bolt them things in place while he an his boys is pointin em the right way on the outside wall. Man from Mechanick Arts stand there with his instruments to tell em when the hour need to strike. Im always inclined to add some silver to my pouch whatever come my way except signin on for shifts. So I go up top an monkey shamble through the works in there. Its clankin mechanism more than soft machine. Gears an wheels an rods an levers an more smaller gears. Ropes an weights an chains an even smaller gears if you look for em. Spinners an handles an scapements an all of it nestled in a iron frame eight feet high. Perched up top is four bell domes bout the size a Child Town helmets an four swing hammers hangin there to tap em for the hours. Upright turnin pole an gear at one corner connects with the overhead shaft that run the length to the steam house. Everthing connected. You wonder how it is that any one can think a all that. Hard to fathom all this widgetry to move two clock hands round.

Withy an his boys is up the ladders on the other side a the wall. They grunt an slide the settin collar for the big hand onto the main drive shaft. Im suppose to hank the screws to a certain mark on it while the hand outside is pointin up. What this means is I shunt the lever so the gears is engaged an chip it round slow to the right point on the shaft. Im doin that. Its movin. Then I hear unholy grindin. Then a yell an shouts an hootin. I cant see nothin where I am so I go round the corner to the steps up behind the sign. Out the little window I see I must a hit the wrong lever an release the dog weight. Or else they told me wrong what to do. That big hand catch the drive gear solid. Withys holdin it so it pull him off the ladder an rotate him backwards round his own clock dial. Hes shoutin. Hangin on the clock hand as it turn. Bare belly pokin out below his shirt an bumpin all the numbers. He keep goin round an round until that dog weight hit the bump stone at the bottom. I got to tell you I enjoy that show longern I need to leanin out the window. Withy lose two whole days there by my countin. Goin backwards through the hours.

Its like this. Say you gots a nice long hank a dove gray chain. Beautiful work. Four of em twisted together dont make up half your little finger. Soft an supple. It flow like water. You may think you got it well coiled in your hand but then the end come free an itll slide an fall like all things fall. The first part will take the next bit with it. Then that pull even harder on the rest. An since it curl like a stream over a rock the whole thingll slide down like water while youre starin at it. Falls at your feet in a little gray puddle.

Well Sir Isaac Newtons apple hit him in the head with such a rumination. Ever thing fall the same no matter what it weigh. Your pendulum of equal length Newton says it swing in equal time no matter what you make it of. Gold or silver. Wood or glass or iron. I think we Iron Boys though we may a proved that last part wrong. Iron Seed it grow up stronger. Iron Apples they go faster when you thow em. Hit harder. Why wouldn a iron pendulum swing a quicker minute. Or would it be a slower one. One or the other. Next thing though your palm be empty an that silky shinin chain is dropped there in the dirt. Or lost or tangled in the greasy gears an lower levers. Cant say a big clock works is a ugly thing. No one think that. It have a beauty thatll even stop you. All them little whirs an nitches is connected in the calculation. Cast a snakin sort a spell to watch it go. Could be why they dont let them works be seen. Enchantment take away the purpose. At Withys theys well hid behind a false wall. Most folk dont even know its false.

Withys pocket clock now thats a cottage wonder. His golden turnip he call it. Most proud of it. All decked around with carved gold leafs an flowers an teakwood chips an locked up with a tender little key. German work. Some time after his big clock is installed he get it. Has special pockets stitched into his trousers an hes sure to pull it out when you there to watch him do it. That little keys attached by a tiny chain no biggern a bit a golden thread. Cant even see the linkwork with my eyes. Germans eyes must be like owls. Withy pinch that key like a dainty nut he pluck to eat. Forty Four say even the dead they want to know about tiny things. That little nub its hardly like a key at all. Chained to the very clock door it open what good is it anyway. Bailiff used to show us children his big iron ring full a long black keys. Thems real clankin keys. They be weighin somethin. Dead folk I bet they care about them things too. Never have a key myself. What would I lock away from what. Withy make me keeper a the factory keys for a time. Even though the place is runnin clock round then an never need to lock up. Withy make me do it anyway. First that clangin four note tune sayin *Dont wait too long. Dont wait too long.* Then them six deep hour bells an there I am gettin folk out the way an heavin the creakin iron clad doors shut. Stick them keys big crenellations in the holes. One lock locked I shouts it out. Thats what Withy tell me. Two locks locked. He says to me you say it Corbel then you know you done it. No danger then a you dreamin through the motions. Thinkin back an wondrin if you done it. He must a knowd I got that tendency. I dont ask him what if I dream the sayin too. So any road them doors is locked an I mark off a minute by the big hand up there while the shifts is massin on both sides. Then I shouts again. One lock unlocked. I unseat the bolt. Two locks unlocked. Pull the latch an creak back the doors. You got to get out the way a the horde a folk come runnin out. They dont go in so fast a course. Twelve hours later I do it all again. Clock say the same thing though one times morn an one times night. For me I dont care. Just another bit a pay. Later the council orders close down the factory at night. Then the lockin up has a meanin. But by then I aint no longer keeper a the keys.

George Cogent Meadows Richard Pilfer Withy the Third. Such a man with such a name let me handle his fabled turnip clock one time. Cover open up like two little doors. Underneath theres six hands on the dial an maybe more. An six smaller circles each got markers a their own. All of em tickin slow in separate confusion. Two dials with moon horns turnin round. Others I cant say. Tell some time somewhere no doubt. Round it all a frilly paintin. Scene a peaceful splendor in a land far away forgot. Pink clouds like that chiffon cloth you might see draped round a ladys bosom. Firelit windows glowin. Archin trees shelter the curvin lane. Rosy golden tint on ever edge no matter how them hands is pointin. I cant stop lookin at it. Its like I been there in that pearly scene. Bundle on my back. I got my own gold key at the bottom a my pocket. Brings a pleasure to my thumb to stroke the edge of it. Fresh nip in the evenin an its one a them warm an lit up houses Im headin for. The one on the left side you can see the most of. Has the brightest glow. Someone in theres waitin for me. Cant quite make her out. I aint countin steps no more. I aint never had a proper home so I cant say its odd to find me one in Withys pocket clock.

Woman waitin for me down cellar. Drawin a pitcher a hazel beer. I come up quiet on the door an pull the key from my pocket where its tangled up with threads an lint an seeds an dirt an bad coin from all the jungly steps an turns an sleepin on the ground thats all behind me now. Put the key in the lock. Turn it silky silent. No sound a slidin bolts or nothin. Door glide open an I smell hot fennel bread. Walk inside an close the door an shunt the bolt. An thats as fars I can get. It all be like another life creep into mine. Or me puttin on a coat that aint my own to stop the shiverin. All this happen in a minute there I figure. Big hand jerk one mark forward. I wernt even lookin at it. I clutch that clock tight till Withy take it from me. My dumb regard must make me no more to him than New Billy. That pretty key though. It bother me somehow. Too little for a proper thumb an finger. Handle on its got a sort a windin maze work you cant see the end of. It keep on curlin small as you can squint. You want to swallow it. See what sprout inside you. But spite a them pink bustle clouds an pretty picture on the so called face Withys turnip knob got a manly heft aint no mistake. Lady wouldn know where to put it. Them Germans dont seem to got a proper notion who its for. Withy wind it up an lock it an slip it back into his special pocket.

When George Withy stare he aint dreamin on a clock dial or countin steps to Unicorn Bridge. He stare at somethin else indeed. He count somethin many zeros far beyond. An yet its right inside his eye. So I dont know nothin. But it all be there in Withys pocket. Close upon his virile member Eddard Weedy might a said. There an up top a the manufactory you got the spinnin clackin clock works with all them motions night an day. You could say theys choppin but no chips is flyin. You could say theys like to the factory shuttles weavin endless yardage. Clock weavin though it aint visible. Finer even than that spider dross linen Withy so proud about. You cant see clock weavin dont mean it aint there though. An nothin weave that fine but got some beauty in the works.

Day like this even the clouds is sleepin up there. Seem like there used to be more mazy motion to a life. I dont mean me. I dont mean wafflin along the road like me with your heels sprangin up little dust puffs. Which in the end them steps whether they be ten thousand to Unicorn Bridge or twenty dozen to the Green Lion with New Billy doggin your heels dont get you anywhere but here an done with it. An I aint talkin about the motions a machines neither. Which ratchet on just fine in their everlastin gobbles as Great Mam might a said. Great Mam she never have to know about six hunnerd sixty spindle to a jenny. About the endless appetite. The alarm go up. Shortage a yarn. Shortage a yarn. Its the constant cry. You can feel it ever time the *Notifier* report the cotton crop sink in a Atlantic storm or pirates longarm the fleet an blunderbuss the bales so they has to be hand plucked. You can feel it in the housin room whenever the stock warden can walk his way across an back without shoutin for someone to move somethin. The appetite aint bein fed.

An Great Mam she somehow know all this. No more skill to spinnin. Hand made aint no longer good an true. Your jolly jobber hes happy. Hes lookin at the buyer not the goods. I think this fellow who say the increasin population will eat its way to doom he may be right. Where do all these people come from any road. Odd dont you think. How they wander in the same time as the manufactory go up. All them wanderers get hired on. But Great Mam when she was pinchin my hand I think that be what she be feelin there. Aint no more skill. Weavin an lace makin. Even my dumb fingers can do it. Talkin bout them cloudy sheep shes sayin machines is suckin up the skill from your finger bones.

I think back to climbin a tree an lookin down from the green sleepy droop of it. Stayin as quiet as that pebble right there. Tippin a bucket full a hard nut apples onto parsons head an hidin like a red indian in the leafage so he never knowd who done it or that any one done it. I think back to them bark boats. Which I imagine one of em might find the sea an then get carried off to India. I mean why not. Aint nobody been able to tell me why it couldn so hap. Made the mistake a talkin to Withy of it. Must a been when he was waxin on bout his ancestral forebears. Sail cloth an bandages from Calcutta. Fabled palace on the banks a the Hoogly. I tell him the story a my bark boats. How I imagine one of em might make its way to India. Where ever that is. On beyond French an Italians somewhere. Ise hopin maybe that he tell me more about how it could happen. I thought Id show him I could think large too. But he put a damper on my glimmer. He start spoutin tides an drift an tropics an anti cyclones an dog latitudes an what not. But all to tell me without sayin so Corbel your childish wish it aint nothin in the Withy world. World where people come from proper people. Instead a from nothin like you. Where people know how to do big things even though they dont have to know because they grandfather knowd an he already done em. Bark boats is what Im talkin about. You know what they say. Give a weaver bird a twig an a leaf an he will weave wonderful things. If you shove a twig into a worm hole in the bark you can stab a big leaf on it for a sail. Sail a course dont do much on the river. Cept some times tip the thing over. That little boatd bang an wallow back an forth rock to rock an bank to bank. Lug lug lug where ever the water go. But I figure it need a sail when it get down the river to the sea. I knowd it be possible to get to India so why couldn I do it with a bark boat. Ever after I been tryin to figure that out. I know I cant but I still dont know why. I think back to runnin cross a field when theys no one after you. I like it when you wasnt goin anywhere but just lyin on your back on some hay after eatin your beans an bread an the fire go out an lookin up an waitin till you see a shootin star. Aint like that now. Unless in Child Town. Snow dont fall the same as it use to neither. Thats a fact. Where do they think the motion in your fingers is gonna go to. You card an rove an pound an draw out a two shilling hank you once done a good days work. No more. Now six hunnerd spindles aint enough. Specially when the housin room is empty. Now it aint real till you see it.

Speed along. Speed along. Thats what that tree right theres sayin with its whippin back an forth. Or some ones sayin that to it. Look. Its the only one. Ones next to it aint movin at all. I walk in the glade an the settin sun may spill out pink under a ledge a cloud an my shadow may shoot out ahead a me twenty yard an more. Speed along. Birds was sayin it also. Such fluttery heart beat little ratchets. Thats just the way they talk. Some may a had a hard time bein clear. Like a angel dont speak about his wings. Speed along. A man who talk fast is a honest man they say. Such a one he dont got time for his tongue to curve his words into little lyin baubles to dangle at you. George Withy might a dandled this philosophy about. He be a fast talker when his steam is up. An it be true so far as it goes. Which is from my lips to the end a my nose. What I think is words runnin forth without a breath between are like numbers growin by zeroes. Steam power can bellows up a thin lie into a fat speech. You may a heard a sermon round here called *Gods Lace Arithmetic.* Been preached an printed up so many times most any one can spin you off a sample till your ears need to take a breath. Sometimes called *Necessity of Rich and Poor.* Here you go.

The size of the demand for lace must intimately link to the quantity of money which the people of a country have to spend on it and when this number is abundant then much lace will of course be bought and if the ready money found in purse and pocket sink then so will sink the purchases of lace by similar degree this much is clear. Yet there will always be some quantity of money vast or somewhat less to expend on lace in so far as the lace itself by its very existence represents a will and a desire of human nature for its own benefit. How then can machinery possibly interfere with such a constant and imperishable desire for something that exists through will and desire. No indeed it can only be a lever and an amplifying pulley for the links of the chain already forged as when for instance the sum we shall propose that the nation expend on lace be one hundred thousand pounds a year for a number of yards we set at five hundred thousand and let us say as well that the making of the lace employs twenty five hundred families. Then we must perforce acknowledge that the lace made by machines amounts to four shillings per yard whereas the lace still stitched by hand adds up to twenty shillings per yard and thus each can see for himself that the effect of breaking a machine even putting aside the cost of its repair not to adduce where the machines have come from in the first instance produces no advantage for the worker as there is only the same one hundred thousand pounds a year to spare for lace. Thus there would be call for and ability to produce only one hundred thousand yards instead of five hundred thousand yards and still there would be the same two thousand and five hundred families employed in lace making at forty pounds a year for each and clearly no improvement in these figures could arise from the destruction of lace machinery whether violent or no because as the quantity of money and the competency of desire for gods fine lace must remain the same with adjustments only according to the population which ever more increases then the existence of the machinery itself cannot possibly do the journeyman any harm but on the contrary the journeyman himself is injured by his injurious behavior to machinery. Since therefore the same mixed sum of money and desire persists in our lace equation then the handmaiden of reason must herself make clear that if machines were to be invented so as to produce lace for half or even one quarter of the present price then by such an improvement there would be a greater quantity sold and wages would remain exactly the same and not a whit lower as is often claimed. So that gods lace arithmetic as I have hereby shown presents the prettiest pattern of constancy like unto the heavens in their own imperturbable and lacelike dominion. One need fear not that machinery and god are opposing forces. Fear not I say and say again. No the two are twined in a never stopping quest for ever greater amounts of perfection. Fear not as we can say together that glory though singular and already perfect to god can be greater to us here below as our divine machines make finer lace and faster lace and more lace. And fear not. The finer and the faster and the more. These are the stepping stones on the way to the kingdom of heaven which takes us awe bestricken straight before the very machineries of god whose numbers of gears and levers interlinked be uncountable. Therefore fear not. They do not and can not and will not compose the number of the beast as spitters and grumblers feel free to say but let us say instead and say a thousand thousand thousand times with me. Gods grace is lace and gods lace is grace.

If you aint memorized such lacy calculations from the fulminatin that pour out of each godly church from Arspittle to Runny Pumps you can find it on the broad sheet Withy have printed up in five thousand copies by his steam press in the time it take to hear it sung. Speed along. Fars I can tell that sermon got no rhyme nor rhythm cept the fear nots in it pressin us to go faster. Like the music master perched atop the piano forte in Maldons parlor. Little wood box. Brass finings an simple works inside also brass. A arrow lever an a key to wind it up like the turnip clock.

An a rod that waggle back an forth remind me a my teachers finger. All in all it was like a clock works stuck inside a obelisk but it got no so called face or hands. I never did quite take the meanin or the purpose of it. New invention brought young Colin Maldon by his father Ben from France. You wind it up an move the arrow back an forth along the etches to make the tock go fast or slow. An this is what you march your music to. Make no sense to me but I cant tell you any clearer what its all about. Young Colin though he love to set it clockin for his lessons. He wind it up tight as a bung plug an push the arrow all the way to the right. Boys they love to pound them keys. Turn your lullaby into a battle march. But Colin do complete his lessons Sarah says an more besides. Speed along. Next thing you know they be hookin up a piano forte to the factory steam engines. Pound its own keys.

They do have a concert in the manufactory once. I dont recall why. Missus Withy no doubt. Eight chamber men out on loan from somewhere. One time only. Withy build a tall stage betwixt the six man frames an the teasel beds. They move the sortin tables out a the way. Withy he pull down them two big power switches with a noontide flourish an all the machinery stop clankin an everbody assemble there to listen. Sudden daytime quiet in that place is weird to hear an you can see the startle of it in the faces. Most folk thronged up cant see much. Chairs in front is only for the fabled few. But sittin there yous almost underneath the stage. Best place is up top a the broad beam over the spinnin mules. Course you never stop ever single thing in a manufactory. Or only one time did that happen in our little history a the world. So now you can hear a tiny *tap tap skreak skreak tap tap skreak skreak* goin dimly underneath the music. Especially in the quiet parts. Like young Colin Maldons music master chip chip chippin away on its own time. Speed along. Wernt many quiet parts though. Mostly them eight fellows was sawin hard to fill the air. Bright sounds like celebration. Dark moans like someone sobbin. An all hinged together by their swayin bodies like some kind a gentle machine. Theys just another part a the manufactory makin sweeter noises. Thats what it seem like to me. But mens motions in a factory aint their own.

Well your hand aint enough an your eye aint enough an your brain aint enough no more. Got to have your steamin machines amplify an multiply till them numbers plunder all arithmetic. On a good clear day like this Id rather say to Withy an to everone. Why fret it. Go out tonight at midnight. Rejoice with the flixweed as it shimmer in the moon light across the factory field. Flixweed it fold up in the day an grow in the dark. Even through the wet slag an forgotten oil spread over the dead earth there. Hail flixweed I say on a good clear day. On a bad clear day I do confess to wishin sometimes Withy an his ilk had long rotted under that dank soil. Turn to black coal skeletons we could set alight to warm our bones. Could be your heart beat faster now too. Speed along. Like a bird wing flutter. Here an gone. One time Desmond Carke find a toad got sliced open on his belly by a whip wire. Desmond pick him up an hold him with a finger mashed down over his bulgy neck pouch. Little head look like your fat high collar lord havin after dinner port. Eyes wide an blinkin an his bellys heavin. You lift open that crosswise flap you can see his little heart pumpin an all them raw shiny gutlets pink an purple pulsin up an down. Perfect glistnin motion like a eye blink. He dont seem in pain. Just astonished. But his turvy heart like all them tiny animals is pit pit pittin fastern you can say. Little leaps fastern Withys turnip clock gears thitterin away. It make me squirmy so I cant say if you can hear it beatin there or no. Desmond want to crack his head open. See if he got the toad stone. But I say hes opened up enough whynt you let him go. So Desmond he pretend to yawn an fling him an the poor thing flop off. I hope he find another toad to lick his belly an heal that cut like they can do.

Carke was once deliverin mice to Timothy Twist for his snakes up to Mechanick Arts. Them experimenters is all excited an runnin round the long slab table cause somethins gone wrong. Usually theys very secretive. But now they got a whole twenty pound African toad laid out there asleep on his back by the special methods an theys speakin openly about the small hose into the dorsal cavity an the stopcock failin which allow the pressure a the so called sublimatory tincture to build too fast an they was worryin that the toad might explode. Which when Carke hear it he take his mice an bag it out a there. I would a too.

Your toads an birds an other little animals is they just machines I wonder. Birds you listen close the sounds they make is some times eerie like a skreak a metal. Is they cryin out a warnin or is they put aloft to mock us. Will we all in time be geared an shafted to the hub of a great machine. Cut you open an you go pulsin on like that. Someone look inside you then fling you off into the flixweed. There may you heal. There may the toads lick you. But what do you know about whats inside a you an what may run the rhythm a your heart.

I keep thinkin why would they name a slow child Ludd. Or name so called King Ludd whoever he may be after a slow child. Whats the fact or import a that name at all. It just be a story. Who get what from it. Mights well his name be Mudd or Thud or Dudd. Sign the name King Ludd now an everones usin it to his own purpose an advantage. As with Robin Hood or Black Annie or Wat Tyler. You could even say Isaac Newton. Or poor King George with leeches suckin his bum an his head in a sack. Who know what these folk really say or do. Only what you hear or read of em. Behind the gilded name is every manner a crossed purposes. Like what pop up in the *Notifier* one Saturday about the king. *No alteration in His Majestys symptoms today* it say in a little box. Next Saturday it say the same. An the next. Then next time it say *His Majesty in the course of the last month is considered to be much worse. On Thursday second past he was understood to be very ill with increased debility. His mental malady on the Wednesday following appeared likewise to be worse. Doctors Symmonds an Monro have been sent for.* Well you be a fool to puzzle over any a that. Them aint the only kingly doctors an aint none agree with the other one. *Notifier* run a little box below the auctions after the Westhoughton hangins. *The prisoners in the city gaol* it says *return their sincere thanks to the mayor and the corporation for the cauldron of coals on Wednesday last which provided a great relief.* I mean what do they want you to think. If they think I believe that then theys ready to be slapped for the pig line race. More like they gots a inch to fill an someone just write whatever they want us to read.

Same with New Billy bein Ned Ludd or bein behind the smashins in some way. Imagine Billy tryin to act the grown man or takin charge or that anyone would think so with his droolin flighty singin. Like when he sing this one it always raise a laugh. Hes so proud of it. Not knowin what it mean an all.

O – I had a maid in Golspie
And – I took her up for tea
I – love that maid a Golspie
But – my numbers thirty three

Now Billy singin his numbers thirty three. That raise a brow or two even though its a old song. Like its concernin the numberin off at the twistins. Or three bein the resumption. The first form. Trine. Triune. Jupiter on his throne an all. An thirty three be double that. But for Billy that dont make sense. Then you have to wonder about New Billy an his horsy. He aint deft enough to ply a sharp tool with them big fingers so he have to have some help makin it. He come one day pullin a frayed rope draggin a wooden horsy bout two feet tall that bumble along after him. Wheels is so knobbly they look like they was gnawed into shape. Horsys a stripped hollow log with four broomstick legs angled off. Billy might a banged that much together I suppose.

But then you look at them counter sunk axles runnin through the hoofs. Who done that. Desmond Carke dont do lathe work. Mill smith over to Dangington swear he dint make em. Too busy to make toys he says. An Mugg Tendon the one eyed stick shaver an thumbless drill man he hate Billy moren he hate god. Mugg wont let it lie. Allus lapsin into sing sing at me he says. Drive me up the pike. Like he were your drooly lovie or somethin he says. Ise tryin to lime up a colchie an he tug me on a shoulder I kick him off *whumm.* Gum him right here an he go down. Stop shut. Get up an go away sobbin an quiverin. Good gone him. Wont come no more na me Mugg says laughin that black laugh. Truth is Mugg he drool as much as Billy. No one know who give that horse to him. Slotted on the front a the log is a thin plank jigged out to a head shape. Snout an smile remind me a Gladden though Im the only one see that. Mane is a fringe a thin leather cords. Eyes is black buttons fastened on to wobble. Boot grease give the rough wood a hairy shine. Bit a Withys new hemp rope for a tail. Your threads snipped an brushed the wrong way to bush it up.

Under that tail a holes drilled in the plug end a the log. Billy point that out to you with that soiled glee he got. You dont know why till he pull the saddle off an drop in six brown stones about the size a bitter booby eggs. Billy jump an squeak an finally calm his self an pull the horse along. Its rollin on them bumpy wheels. Must be some gearin an a pulley belt an slots inside that move them stones so one by one they drop out from that bung hole. Thop thop thop there on the ground like turds scared out of a leapin deer. New Billy a course he cant get enough a this an load up that poor horsy over an over with them six stone shits. Trojan Horsy. Dont know how he ever hear a that. Billy come up to me holdin a long curl a bouncy wire. He make me take one end. Cant think of a good reason to say no. He shake it out an shove the other end into the bung hole. *Zhzhzhzhzhzh.* He make a big buzzin through his teeth an let the wire drop in the dirt. Then he grab horsy by the handle an roll him along fast as he can on them knobbly wheels. *Raaangg raaangg* he says an run cross the lane an round the corner an back down Chapel Way while I stand there still holdin that damn wire. He come back up to me to do it again but I let my end drop. You dont need me I says. His face cloud over an I think how old is he. When hes disappointed he look like a older man whos still a baby. Yet his features aint enough to fill his face. Somethin missin somewhere. What you doin Billy I says. Get the *gaaahh* he says. Mister Withy he give me the *gaaahh.* It go in there. Make horsy run fast. Whats the *gaaahh* Billy I says. The *grrrrh* he says. I dont know what is the *grrrrh* I says. He start stampin. Get that cloud a impatience over him that make people do things for him they shouldn. *Grrrrh* he says. *Gaaahh.* Wheel go round he says. He stick his wiggled end a the wire in the hole an shake it. *Zhzhzhzhz.* Horsy run he says. An off he go with it rollin an tumblin behind him.

Trojan Horsy. King Ludd. New Billy. I aint sayin this or that or what become a Saint Stephens garter. But you go ahead an try to put things together when theys happenin all around you. An what order things be in. An what causes what. There do be seventy two testified kings a this isle even before the real King

Ludd. Seventy two or seventy four. Depend on if you say Ferrex an Porrex is two or one. Samewise Belinus an Brennius. Theys twinned together in the kingly lists so may be they share a crown some how. I never seed a double headed crown but why not. Brutus come first. Everone know that. Though how do you know it. It be told to you or you see the list in a book an they make you recite it top to bottom. Brutus be the one who come here from Troy. He build Trinovantum which they say is where Big Town is today an reign there twenty three years. Then it all be somewhat cloudy down the page to Gwendolen who reign fifteen years an Mempricius twenty years. Then Brutus Greenshield twelve years. Rud Hud Hudibras thirty nine years. Bladud twenty. Mad Leir sixty an all that mess you still hear about. Queen Cordelia she reign five years only an a goodly thing I reckon. Many more I dont recall come after. Once upon a time I knowd em all. Kings an years. Kings an years. They make you learn it like you cant have the names without the numbers. I always liked the great Dunvallo Molmutius who seem to be mostly forgot. Reigned forty years. Theys a song about him though I cant think of it right now. *Here come the great Dunvallo. As deep as he is shallow.* Then there be the likes a Marganus. Royal Runo. Urianus. An a course theres Bledudo. Some time later you get Archmail. Eldol. Penessil. Start to sound like recitin the names a the stars. Pir an then Capoir. Sound like some French get in there. Then Heli forty years an finally old King Ludd. Ludd they say he build the golden walls an ramps made out a red an white sardonyx all round Trinovantum. Which is why it be later called Ludds Town. Ludds brother Cassivelaunus he fight Big Caesar hand to hand though where an when is of some confutation.

But the important thing is the unbroken line from Troy to here. Like your plant come out of a seed an then your seed come out a the plant an then your plant come out a the seed an on an on like that without end or beginnin amen. Like day an night. The bird or the egg. Which come first. You may say everthing start with the defeat a Troy but why do you say that. Ludds men may want to say the line a Ludd survive from olden times. What Iron Boys want to say is that Iron Seed is all you need. So Billy says Withy give him the *Gaaahh* to make his horsy run. But this wire he put to Trojan Horsys bung hole. Barrel top speaker back at Fool Fair tell about the camel who shit while crossin the river. Camel turn round an says *I see what was behind me is now before me.* The meanin a this story is that those of low estate now rule. World turned up side down an all. Well clock handsll tell you that much. Aint hard to find better terpretation. What you put inside you poop back out an there you got the shape a things to come. Everbody know it but fewll spend the time it takes to properly scry their shits. But think a all the shits you sank on this dim earth from the time youre up an trottin. Dark backward of you. Endless broken smelly tail bound to tell a story of its own dont you think.

Say you eat the same thing ever day for the week. Me it once might a been Brindles sour loaf with them thick stripes a onion curd folded in. Slop some pigberry jam on it an nothin else I swear. A loaf a day. Pints a beer a course. Branch water or a dip from the bucket when Gladden need a drink. Stale ends a last weeks loaf you can wipe your arse with. Peel off the sharp crust an that good cross grainll keep you clean. Now youd expect if you put the same brown loaf in you ever day that a like brown loafd come out. But no. One day its flat glowin tan folds back an forth but still connected in one long wrinkly flop. Next day its dark hard bombs bounce off each other an roll in the ditch one two three four like Billys Trojan Horsy. Then you may get two long curls lie side by side like sleepin stoats. Or roundy mounds like your ladys bustle mushrooms. Shape an number. Thats the rule in divination. You got to look at it good an hard without thinkin too much. Whether it be massy an loud when it plump out like a tuba horn or skrinched out slim in little grunts. Or straight log shits like George Withys. Or rooty rank an spreadin like a deep forest swamp. Or dark an thin an fast like a ink snake into the scrub. One time I had a nine foot earthworm shoot out an curl up like in a basket. Course theres days you poop in places you cant reckon from. When it aint steamin there on flattish ground or in what catch all you may be squattin over. I hear theys a fancy new tin trough in the water closet at court house hall. John Gwilt tell me it got water runnin from a spill pipe on to a dump tray with a chain. I aint tried that yet. Thatd give you a good shit scryin platform.

You got to wonder about King George. Some say it be the distillations of his blocked up shits which affect the workins a the regal brain. Royal doctors try blisters on his scalp an feet to draw the poison up or down. Penny lucre for a purge an swamp mallow to slump him in a stupor. Leeches on his bum. Windows wide at night. Cold black food. Antimony to bring the fevers. Doctors hang him up side down. Stretch him on the rack. Anvils on his gut. Tie his hands behind an rub his belly on a oak tree. Shove a funnel up his arse an pour in what have you. All in vain they say to dislodge that stinkin dead rock clut in there. The question be if they aint able to divinate the royal shits then whos in command a whats to come. You think a king need such signs moren most folk. But this king just wave his arms like a maniac an howl like a dog. You dont read it in the *Notifier* but such was seen an sweared to by those who know.

Where was we. Your spewin poop. That predict nothin but confusion. Best thing is when first come a hard piece. Then the soft one nextll tell you what you need to know if you scan it quick before it slump too much. Some days it look like a fat wet stick broke in two pieces. Then you want to figure the so called ratio. Or if they lean together like kindlin you count the fissures in the sides. It aint a single meanin like that Dream Book Maggie Moats is always readin. *If you dream of a bird that flies out of a window you will get what you wish or else the thing after.* Or Maggies Number Book. Suppose you got six sheep in a meadow an two wander off. *Six is the number pertaining to mothers. Two is the number of division yet it is complete. Your mother will not recover from her illness but will be received into heaven.* With shit your answers aint mechanical like that. You poop out three puppy tails for instance. They may be sayin wait for the third offer to come your way but it may be anything to do with three. Or which direction do they curl. It may be indicatin what way to turn at a three road cross or it may be three smiles or three frowns you need to pay attention to. You got to sniff it out yourself. Aint no book gonna tell you. One weird mornin a long time ago I drop a fat wet sausage like to have a face at either end. One look like Withy an one look like. Well I wont tell you. What you supposed to think when that come out a your arse. Aint reckoned that one yet.

Of all the divinations known to man the birds has ever tallied first. At least till they start speakin speech. Which complicate the jurisdiction. Maggie Moats tell me about a lady she knowd who dream she find a nest a seven finches an thats how many children she later have by the second husband. She didn know him when she have the dream but his name turn out to be Finch. You cant dream only what you want to though. I make a little pillow from a bag full a meadow bells and royal cuntwig an lay my head on it an try an dream a Silvy but it dont work like that.

Im feelin spooly today some reason. Like them spools that come unwinded when you forget the foot brake on the bobbin spindle. Tangles all over the floor. So Ill tell you bout the night a the fabled stockin dance. Bout wearin trousers on your head. Bout salutin those who fart. Them mooly customs is born all on one night. Still alive an so much else is gone. So be it. No one knows whatll live an why. It were a night had many nights in it. You can feel the prickles early. Torn clouds over Wise Crag just after dark lit up by lightnin scraps. No thunder. Trees fly back an forth discomfited. You know somethins brewin. Mid November but uncanny warm. World swingin back an forth on the pivot a that night. Could a gone any direction. Thats what it seem like. Course this just be the old Green Lion. It wernt the world. Unless Withy be proven true. *Not this valley but the world.* Night feel large enough when you see such things you never seed before.

So Im come from Bastford. Shouts an crashin half a mile ahead spill out the ever slammin door. Gibbous moon follow me down the road an I dont want it to. Mind me of the skull glowin in the wooden box which Miss Bird snap down on my fingers on Nut Crack Night. She shut it fore I can tell what it is light up that skull in there an make it laugh like that. I still see Miss Birds head tiltin back an forth just like a bird an shes laughin too. They all try to scare me in that school when I first get brung here. But this night my Gladden hes pullin me on my cart an I come up under the walnut trees by Whisker Floss. Pass under Black Woppers eyes. Them witchy canker whorls where the two limbs was sawed off to let the tall carts turn onto the new road to the factory. Gladdens smilin to get there cause he know I be givin him some sugar lumps. I get up to the yard an some haunt come over me. Coaches traps an carts outside. Whose is they. Horses an dogs I dont seem to know em. Jolly strangers goin in an comin out. The two windows look like golden eyes. Flappin curtains let out a pretty light. Lion on the sign board look fresh painted under the lamp. Even frisky. Prancin on his hind legs with his two green paws crossed in the air.

I go inside theres Desmond Carke. Desmond hes just signed that letter to the *Notifier* on the misery in the weavin trades. John Gwilt hes there. Pank House. Ben an Sarah Maldon. George Withy. Jane his wife. Rose Stonewarden. Maggie Moats an Barley Moats. Many strangers also. Moren usual fill the place. Drinkin spillin stompin squawkin all over cept for Sarah an Missus Withy. Someone with his neck stretched back is singin about Napoleon.

Boney fingers every pie
And he will eat them by and by

Too warm by the fire. Just across the corner from the window Carke an Gwilt theys set up a game a draughts. Desmond he put two fingers in the air to call for pints an thow a smooch at Cecily cross the room. Its on my slate he says if I dont crown three before your first. Some times folk thow things at Cecily make her dodge just to get a curse out a her. Lots a shoutin from the kitchen. Cheese an jam. Mustard an pickles. Shanks an vinegar. Bowls an platters clatterin. Muffled runnin back an forth behind the wall. I favor the Dundee opening Gwilt warn Desmond with some pomposity. Bettern none at all Carke says. Chidin his delay but Gwilt dont hear the edge.

Above the game a Child Town waif is sleepin on the shelf. Head up against a haunch. Arm dangle down. Wild hair. Grain sack someone thow over him for a blanket. Feet about to kick a jar a plums. Dreamin through the racket in there. Just the fact that there can yet be such a sleep in such a world. Be that a blessin or a curse. Them Child Town rascals is used to noise. So many of em workin in the factory. An then the racket of em always throwin stones an slappin swords an theres the squallin a the infants that keep gettin born or dropped off there. An the fights. But when he stir an rub his eyes a couple a potatoes tumble off the shelf an devastate the board. Them pieces roll not only where you think they should but into far corners an even underneath a piece a carpet. Has to be gremlins. Chalk it up as Ludds game says Carke. Who is that child up there says Gwilt but dont seem to want a answer. That child he wake up like a dog an never think a what it was he dream. Like he never dream at all. May be thats good if its a bad dream. But where do that dream go. An what if it be a good dream he forget. What would it mean.

Any road Withy hes tryin to maintain the center of attention despite the wildness all about. Man is made he says to rise up on his two hind feet. Unlike the animals. Follow my reasoning if you can. This upward striving is in truth the commandment of the Lord to work for daily bread. Not crawl along the ground grubbing shoots an simples. Shoot grubbin aint solely for the beast Carke shout. I do shoot grubbin some myself. An now he pumps his self across the floor with his hands on his boot heels like some dancin troll. Folk at the Lion they love a ruction an now things start to fly along. Withy he attempt to claim lost ground while Carke attempt a handstand though none too steady.

The craft of man can so much imitate the artifice of nature Withy says that it can make an artificial animal. The French have made a mechanical shitting duck he says. As only they would think to do. And now by heavens mercy the snarking Desmond Carke will demonstrate his arse upon his shoulders as in the Masque of Shame. By this time Carkes collapsed an Cecilys poured a pint over his head. Withy marches on behind his thought platoons. In our enlightened time he says what would the next step be. Naught but the artificial man. He wave his arms an stamp his legs like some jack giant trampin down the hill. In a manufactory such as my own he says we produce more with machines than with our hands. More work more goods more pay thats always true. One plus one plus one he says. Thats the chain of logic gentlemen. Machinell amplify your work and all the worker do is match the movements of machines. But tomorrow we shall all have heads made of gears and spindles turned by steam to tell our mechanick fingers and feet just what to do and when to do it. This new automaton my friends is artificial life. Then I can devote myself to my ballooning and oversee the factory from the air instead of from my chair.

John Gwilts inspired by Withys expostulations. As well as three quick pints by my accountin. He move his long face right towards Withys table. Pullin off his boots along the way he knock over his chair an force Cecily into a cossack dance. Its no large thing Withy says. What is a heart but a pendulum. What are nerves but pulley belts. What are joints but interlocking gears. What is fat but grease. What is muscle but a piston pumping up and down. What are thoughts but wheels inside of wheels. Gwilt he lift his foot right up to Withys face. See this here stockin he says. Appears I must says Withy as youve kicked my plate into my dear wifes lap. This here stockin Gwilt says. It go all the way up to my knee. Words as true says Withy are not spoken every day. He pinch Gwilts toe there in the air. Gwilt jerk back an spin an stamp an hop to keep from fallin. But he manage to hold his leg high up an even almost tickle Withys nostril. An witness this Gwilt says. This stockin never never never will it fall down round my ankle. At each never he lift his leg a little higher. He huff an puff an you know by that his clerkship at the factory is a sittin job. Hoppin round on his other heel he gasp it out. My dear momma make em. Own hands. Rough silk. She give em to me. Christmas time. Apple in each one. See the little doodad here. Broidery has my nitials. Done by hand. J G see there. Look what else. The year. You see how old. These stockins thirty year. Never need one stitch a mendin.

Withy hes drawed back in disgust behind his wife. Hands on her shoulders watchin this display. As much as hes always shoutin on a box shes always stuck upright an silent in a chair. Amusin to see him tryin to hide as he issue his retort. From the stench he says I do believe you never take em off. Any but the Mayor of Guzzledom knows it. If youre moving fast enough your stockings will fall down. Your stockings John Gwilt are up around your knees because you are a layabout. A shirker and a wastrel I would not waste my horse whip on. Ive been watching you and you are sacked. Whats more I knew your mother. She was fair shod by Napoleons personal bootmaker. Gwilt cant let this pass. Buy my Dutch biscuits he croak out to a snarly mixture a laughin at him an laughin with him. Now his feets on the ground an his fists is curlin. Withy brushes his self off an sits down an says with the brass unction of all his Cogent Meadows Richard Pilfer Withy blood, *My bellows I would never lend but you may sit by my fire and blow.*

Well it wernt far from this to trousers on the head. They was a new kind a trou sported then. Come up from Big Town. Become the style of many young folk here about. Bagged out legs. Chopped off short up the shin. Slung low about the hip bones. Theres a jest you hear about em. Them new trou are not waisted on the young. W A I S T. Gwilt wears em in spite a bein too old for em. You falling on your bum in such a guise Withy says. Why dont you wear them fancy trousers on your head. Despite the laughter Gwilt he have his dignity to keep. So he pull hisself up all sober sides an button by button he take his trou off then an there to Missus Withys somewhat doe eyed consternation. Though a course Gwilt got dingy leggins underneath. He tie the waist band round his head just so. Wide legs hangin down his back like royal banners. There he stand like he wear that head dress every day. Must be the wild iron look in his eye but no one say a word. Carke shout somethin lewd but it fall flat. People tell you many things about that night but I tell you the truth. Trou head fashion was born right there at George Withys suggestion. I do think he regret it for a while since he wernt up an runnin with a line. But hes quick to see them numbers dance. Soon enough the newest trou aint even made for your legs. It was Withy create the fancy patch work trou. Allowin much flooreage to be resurrected. Useless scraps patched together be naught but profit. Dont even have to be stitched together right. But this stockin dance. Gwilts there with his trousers on his head an Withys up an friendly again with his mug a ale an everbodys dancin round one foot in the air an pullin at their stockins. Shoutin an singin in rhythm. *Never. Never. Never. Will it. Fall. Fall. Fall.*

Pank he just been sittin back through all of it. That be his way. Not one to put trousers on his head. No one ever know his thinkin. He say first this thing then another an you believe it all. Hes disappearin more than hes appearin. So it were unbelike hisself to jump the moment. He sneak up from behind though Gwilt dint take much sneakin. Just a wee tug sideways on his flappin trou head legs an he come down hard an flat. Bust a big buzzin fart when he hit the ground. Withy jump to stand before him with a military posture. I salute you sir he says clickin his heels the way they all do now. An thats how come the custom of salutin those who fart. Gwilt was not sacked. Thats just a game they has.

First a the so called trou heads is those folk who chum up around John Gwilt. His friends an those who respect his strict position with the men. He be one a them able to keep his tongue in his pocket where he can pinch it to keep quiet. Gwilts the former master of a household shop up to Six Acres. Ten twelve hand frames. Comin a the factory turn him out. Him an many more. Johns quick to line up at the gate though. Never question it. Yet he hold his head up when they others droop em down. Loyal opposition you might say. But come the fateful fork you cant take both ways can you. *Like unto the tracks of a cart one wheel of iron and one wheel of mahogany. But the cart shall one day come asunder. The two wheels shall diverge. The tracks shall part and go their separate ways.*

Theres somethin wrong with me. You must know that by now. Not just a lack a legs. I mean behind the eyes. Somethin missin or else could be somethin extra not put in right. Somethin wrong up here. Well that be said a lots a folk. Lalloway. New Billy. Some truth to that. You open them up somethin sure to be rattlin around in a empty place in them folks heads. Me its more peculiar. I got all the thoughts I want but they go off round the corner. Then round another. Could be Im like Billys Trojan Horsy. Brain poopin out pebbles like a mechanical clock. But whos loadin the hopper. Id pay somethin to learn that. I remember a shiverin day at the sea shore. Sittin on the rock with a man. Sad sea birds they squeal an circle over head an try to warn me. My shiverin an shakin wake me up from some safe place where I be warm an dreamin. I try an remember that dream but I never do. The way that man talk to me he must think I understand him. But I dont understand him. An I wish I did cause it might explain a large amount. My best an foremost thought is to tell you a the Iron Apples an the Iron Boys. An how it come to be. An all things connected with it. An you see what happen. One thing an another but not in proper order. Wish I could lay it all out like a story. Like Black Wopper. Once upon a time. It aint your time an it aint my time but time for me to tell you thus an so an then an that an now the end an sleepy time. My mind it dont move along like that. Much as I try to stick it to the gist. Wont do it. How do you know what is the gist. Or could be somethin bout it dont want to be told.

Nancy poor thing. She never knowd a my conversin with the birds. Id a liked her to know. She have a place for everthing an everthing was jig right with her as long as she have it in a place. She would a understood. Even moren me. Not like Silvy who everthing be quizzical to or even wrong. Nancy used to put her thumbs against her fingers an peck em like two beaks upon my neck. In front under the jaw. Protectin herself. Keepin me from kissin her. Shes doin them beaks on me an I grab her hands an hold em behind her an plant a big long kiss. We both sink deep into that one. An it be the only time. Deepest I ever had though. Enough to last all this while. Cause I can still sink back into it. Kissin Nancy was like a pelican comin down in the water. Fast an slow. Clumsy an delicate. Just before landin you get that backward chuffin an flappin of wings. Then calm again like it never happen. Mama didn treat her softly brushin that thick hair. Papa couldn see it. Nancys throats stretched back like that toad Desmond Carke find. I can hear her call my name. Low voice an teeth tight. Not bein able to twist up an look at me. Corbel she says with her eyes shut but I can see em movin underneath. An then she give up an slump when I dont answer. She must a knowd. An poor blind papa there. Smilin off his chair in some direction. Nancy jerk forward sayin ow ow an her bobbers under her blouse theys bouncin like flesh bags that aint connected to nothin. Some kind a emptiness in there now instead a fullness. My heart for sure right then it hang heavy as a wooden clog on a birds leg.

So you see what Im sayin. Aint in me to keep a straight path. Look over there. Barrel full a flour. Exact color of Maggies milk cow round the udder. How you get from high sproutin wheat to fluffy flour. I mean miller know that but who tell him. His father but who tell him. His father but who tell him. How do the first one know what to do to get from them thin wavin stalks to good arse wipin bread. What straight line is that I ask you.

That cold sea shores the first thing I recall. Wave on wave on wave an nothin happen. Sea water aint no mirror like the mill pond. No glimmer in them gray soapy bobs an oily motions. *Loom.* I recall there was a lady choked up sobbin then. All wrapped up like me in these old scarves. Is that my mama I always wonder. Her dream she told me of. Her little baby come to life again. It aint dead. It just be so cold she says. Cold an now its curled up there against her heavin breast. She take it close up to the fire wrapped in its stained swaddlin cloth. Baby start to bunch up cryin an its little fist beat on its face an its alive. Its alive. An then she wake up an find no baby. Not hers nor anothers. Hardest part is when she knit her little babe a crown she call it. Sewed with tiny tinkle bells an feathers. But there aint no babe. An shes all drooped over in her dirty red cloak made out a sackin cause she been so sickly. I think about that little thing alive in her arms back in the safety of a dream. How dreams is better some times than the world you wake to. The world do got a solid sameness you can knock on. Some times that be good an some times not so good. Well now you see my problem. What am I talkin about. I dont even know. You go on an take your lunch.

Like I dont know if you ever seed this. It gots to be connected with what wes doin. Youre sittin lookin at a apple tree an a apple fall to the ground while you watch. *Tump.* Just like that. An somethin true just been spoke. As with Sir Isaac Newton in his orchard.

In the evenin a that hot August day. Number a that year be sixteen an sixty six. Significant dont you think. Sir Isaac sit up on his hill an face back down to his house. His college is shut on account a the plague. Dry summer so his trees is full a wrinkled apples. Stems is loose an brittle an a shrivel sink into em even before the blush come on. Moons near full an up at dusk like its been there waitin always. An Newton they say hes contemplatin fluxions. Sound like somethin King Georges doctors might a tried to ease his gutly pains. Fluxions though is numbers have to do with curvin things. Most a your numbers be curvin numbers come to that. Them numbers tell Sir Isaac how the spirit sink to act upon a body in proportion to the distance an the density of it. How the particles a ether push on the surfaces. So Newton you can see his eyelids sunk but not quite closed. Hot country evenin. Nothin back then like the racket all round everthing today an them belt wheels squeakin through the night. His wig is on his little table with the water pitcher. Then the apple tump there by his feet which is stretched out in white stockins an layin on a little pink pillow under the famous tree. That apple it fall right past the moon there in his sight. An Sir Isaac see that the moon instead a risin like you think it is is ever fallin like that apple. Fallin round the earth. Not ever hittin it. Cause it curve to the side as fast as it fall an so it go round an round forever. Old moon she look down on you through ever phase an season. The traction of her gaze be like a lode stone.

It were a apple that our eye beguile
Yet wernt no apple that our soul defile
To eat a iron apple darks the blood
Sweet revelation bitten does us good
Spit the seed an juice upon the dove
An eat the apple who art sick a love

I wonder what precisely we was doin with our seeds. Pank he should a told me what was what. If you know what you are doin youll do it better. Thats what I think. But that wernt his way. He like to keep his secrets.

All my walkin seem distant from me now. One day some time ago Im ramblin along with Milky. That lad from Child Town who Eddard Weedy talk about the comet to. Who knows what them children want. Ise in a hurry but he fall in with me an somehow keep up though he have to stride three for two an a extra skip ever so often. Most a them childrens in an out a factory work. Round the sortin table you get Dick today an Giles tomorrow an Susie the day after. Young as eight or six now they be put in as a yarn winder or a stockin seamer. Even younger they be thread pickers or bobbin minders or bag stuffers. Child Towns always gonna be there. Whos your mum lad. Whos your daddy missy. Whats your name. Where you from. You ask all that but you get nothin or lies. They gots a code. So I dont ask. Me an this lad wes walkin along silent for a while. Then he up an speak like a bright boy. What is death Mister

Penner. How you know my name I says. We know all the folk who be right an give us stuff or do things. I never give you nothin or do nothin I says. He let that pass with a twig in his mouth. Tryin to spit like a man. Death I says. I can tell you what the birds say about it. Thats why you come to me aint it. He look up an his face is shinin white an red from a special scrubbin. Hair combed back wet so you can see the dirt he didn find on the side a his neck an the scabby stuff behind the ears. Nothin I says. Birds say nothin on it. Alls I know is this I says. Body lay down tired one day. Stiller than you can stay when youre dizzy lookin at the clouds after spinnin or even when youre hidin from a beatin. That little thing inside I says. You know it. Tiniest feather you can picture floatin on the air. Tinier than that. Cant even see it. Float out so quiet nobody notice. Float out straight on a secret breath from inside your nose. Goin to a place it dont want to come back from. Peaceful place I says. So peaceful they call it the land a milk and honey. But you dont even want milk an honey. You dont need it.

We walk on for a while. Three for two an a extra skip ever so often. How do you know where to go he says. I says you know inside. Everbody know. Aint no other place to go. Sometimes you know when. Sometimes yous whispered a secret to I says. What about the bad place he says. Gunny says bad people go to a bad place. Well thats just wrong I says. Aint no bad place. Everthing in one place. May be bad people there like here I says. But everbody go to the same place. Whos Gunny I says. He keep walkin lookin down an I see a tear drip off his eyelash onto his cheek. But that lad he command a stern gulp an he swallow it all back an scuff it into the dirt. I dont want her to go he says. I want to go with her. Soon I start mouthin the same damn toothless mush thats all you ever hear anyone say to a child. She go when its time to go I says. Like all of us. When its your time youll go find her. She be waitin for you. I want to go with her now he says. Mister Penner can you tell me its my time to go an where to go. No I cant do that I says. It have to come from inside. From somewhere else. Not from me I says. Well you want to do good. You dont want to do bad. But its hard to know what to tell a young lad. When you run out a things to keep quiet about is when you get stupid so a course I keep talkin. Listen here I says. You see that hedgerow. He nod. You might walk by that hedgerow I says day up day back all summer long. Come autumn them little leaves turn yellow. Some of em fall off. You walk by you can make out some a whats behind.

Then them leaves turn brown. Wind come up an more blow off an you can see a little more I says. One winter day you see right through it. See things you never seed before. Like that old iron claw lie there rustin. An that beat up crate they brung the rifles in. It be like that. Then just to taunt me a bird pierce out somewhere near though you cant see him. *Unique.*

Unique. But the boy he just keep walkin an dont take it in or maybe he dont got a ear for French. French syllables get me excited even before Silvy. A course I cant tell if such a word as *unique* got aught to do with us or not. Birds fly about so much theys always bringin scraps from afar. Im thinkin I should talk to Ben Maldon about if he think our birds an French birds is communicatin. But I dont trust him. Hes got moren two opposite things goin hisself.

Mister Penner Milky says an I wonder what it is that make him so polite with me. That aint a Child Town trait. Rude an ready at you most times they all is. I dont like my name he says. They laugh at me. Will you make a new one for me. Well you dont just make up a name I says. Or start to say but then think better on it. Who says you dont. I never name no one except for callin Silvy Little Mink once when she was all wrapped round my neck with her legs stuck up a tree. Rat Tail Jack he come to me an already gots his name. An Gladden I just shorten it from Gladiator. But a name for this lad who need a new name. Look I says. Why dont you take me to meet Gunny. His head hang down so far I know whats comin. Its them Child Town lies. There aint no Gunny he says. Just my sister. Lets go see your sister then I says. She an Ill make you up a name. There is a Gunny he says. Gunny dont talk to me. He just laugh at me. Push my face down in the dirt. What about your sister I says. I aint got a sister no more he says. She left with a fellow to have a baby. I put my hand on the poor lads shoulder though its hard to walk that way bouncin up an down like differnt horses. What else can you do. Child Town liesll wear you out.

In them weeks before the big attack on Withys there was your little unplanned smashins here an yon. First frame breakins wernt much to em though. Just quick eruptions in the general upset. Desmond Carke call em shakins not breakins. George Withy himself it was who broadcast the rumor theres about to be a job on Bastford. Now it look like Bastford be the start of it. Desmond he say Withy want to place us at Bastford by tellin us about it. That dont seem right though. He didn think like that. Withys the one keep John Gwilt from the sheriff. Hes just speakin out in disbelief. Tryin to win us to his side. Wants a place for you in his perfect world. But none the less the word is goin round. Smashin comin down in Bastford on the Friday. An under thats the notion we might expect the same right here. Only reason Withy could want some man jack over to Bastford is as a spy. But he didn whisper any such thing to any one fars I know.

So Thursday night Im trundlin along on my cart like usual. I aint haulin nothin much those days though Im always goin from here to somewhere else an back. Me an Gladdens bumpin over Humpleback down to Little Bastford close on sunrise. I love that low trumpet of the sun comin up. First your orange. Then your pink. Then yellow like you might hear it. Then some how its the blue or white or gray day itself an you already forgot about the dawn. Three fellows I dont know ask me for a ride at the crest. On the way down they cajole or convince me to come with em. At the bottom I stop an tie up Gladden with a bucket a water an we break into the first cellar we find that aint bein watched. In fact we has our pick. Second third an fourth is open for the takin. Anything we can stow in a bag to thow in a hurry. Folk is scared the one fellow says. He wont look at you when he talk. Scared a what I says. Whats in the *Notifier* he says. They think we breakin in to kill em. Leave their cellars open to distract us he says. I try to tell him even smart folkll spew back what they read without thinkin. *Notifier* can say frame breakers drag off a factory master an slit his throat. Or it can say King Ludd find a lost gold ring when he slit the belly of a fish. After folk hear *Gods Lace Is Grace* three four times be like marble hit a marble. Newtons law or thereabouts. Menll mumble to themselves I dont know much but must be true that the more fine silkeen cloth chump out a the machines the more coin clink in my cup. I got me a family. I gots to work faster now. They be talkin to themselves but the words is anothers. Most a what folk do aint more sensible than that. Mights well be cogs in a machine like old Sheppey said. Which make me wonder. Are we copyin the motions a machines or is they simply mimickin us only doin it a hunnerd time faster. Makin fun on us like a bad jape. I mean theys ever more people in our little world. Why does we got to work faster.

Down in the square everone was passin out cobs an littlins. Someone roll up a barrow a taters an then another full a rocks. Them taters some start eaten em an the ladies is sayin they aint cooked theys for thowin. I see a sharp fellow rubbin tater dust on a rock an tryin to get a Child Town lad to bite it. I wernt sure about thowin apples. Not right thowin good Wicks Pippins or Plush Regals is my thought. Good ones too from last year. Before the bad cider an all. A tater in your hand though. You feel the bumps on it like on your head. One bump this taters got you hold it right is the one be number thirty two. Memory. Right around your temple. I feel it with my middle finger like its already hittin the guard I see walkin by the main gate. It was Tommy Meacham. I fling that tater without thinkin an it do hit him right on that bump. Im laughin cause he be certain to remember it. Then he look my way with a evil glare. I can see black powder in his eyes so I stop smilin an slink away.

Eat me a apple
Swallow a seed
See the smoke risin
Watch a man bleed

Good thing he dont know me. Theys nine other guards I can count. Armed with pike hammers an long hatchets like we is. Plus your rough an ready stakes an timber an assorted metal bolts an pipes an junk. One mans on the roof with a rifle but he seem afraid a gettin hit an keep a flinchin this way an that an almost tumblin off the edge. A few rocks an taters an apples come at him an hes gone. A few more conk the guards outside an they slip away as well. One of em even sidle over to our side. Probly had a hungry eye on them taters. Then a sun beam strike them hundreds a window panes at once an like a signal them windows is crashed through quick an frames is smashed an cloth piles burnt an a Ludd note left. I dint do anything that time but hit Tommy Meacham with the tater.

I dont know who it was set up the Bastford smashin an sign the Ludd note. None of em is caught. Soon enough the battles grow fierce all over. Some Luddish an some no name put to em. An the arse wipe *Notifier* aint only scarin folk out a their cellars. Theys mixin everthing up. True an rumor an false alarum all in a big stew. Like whats printed about the Glossop smashin. *Three professing followers of the false and vile oathing King known as Ludd considered to be provoker in this shire of the rebellious risings against our fine lace makers and the stocking trade profitable to all good men were set upon the pillories. With them were three others so suspected who were brought into the town from Spital Byfields blindfold on horse back with their faces laid upon the horses tails and waste paper tied about their heads. This by decree of the star chamber convoked October last at*

Assingham by the assistant to the lord treasurer under orders of the Luddite emergency. That aint the half.

Round this time I start thinkin birds is degeneratin. Peck an poop an peck an poop is all they do. Once in a while a simple minded tweet or chirp. Nary a song. An no good word come out of em no more. As if they aint got no idea a the prophetic glory a their nature. Or even the charm a their unkempt flyin mischief. Now days they dont bother to lift a fatty wing. Just a low chucklin as they waddle round. Not even waddle. I seen one stare right straight into a rollin coach wheel that crush him with a pop. He dont seem to care. Sweet little one axle cabriolet on springs that win a prize for how close it can turn. Little coach wernt hardly movin an that bird I seed him just standin there in front a that wheel not even lookin. The eyes a them speechless birds is ironless seeds. Aint no magnetism there no more. So hes just a blowsy dolt of a little white feather ball an he give way with a toothy crunch a his breast bones an a fine spray a crimson driplets. Right across the white frill hem a the dress that lady in the coach is sportin. She cry out mortally upset an dabbin at it. But its a beauty in its way. As if a wand had spangled her with tiny blood jewels. *Like a fool to the stocks* the Black Book say. *So a bird hasten to the snare an dont know it is for his life. But two sparrows be sold for a farthing an aint one fall dead on the ground without your father* somethin or other. Well that dont be true no more if it ever was. Birds now be all replaceable. Harsh thing to say. *Replaceable. Replaceable.* That word dont really sound right. Till then I never seen her kind a lady. An never since. What she wear an the sound a her voice is rich and strange to haunt you. An her black hair all scalloped up an wove with glitter an silver cord. An the green stone in gold twaddles hangin at her robust throat. She just look at me in my now I see rude cart sittin there goin the other way like I be the one spatter the blood on her. Then with a whip crack theys gone a clatterin away in the ruts. There be more gradations a ladies than gents for sure an dur. Why is that.

The Isaac Newton was the public house up by Six Acres at the flint road. Thats where we meet up before our big attack. First time I come there I had walked eighteen miles from the other side a Bastford Bridge. I was younger then a course. But it were a flat straight road an it were one a them days when you be given plenty to do it with but nothing to do. Could a walked on into town. But it had got blowy an was spittin rain my last two miles. The Newton loom up out a the mist with a creamy glow. Look all plush an invitin like it be the Cow an Candlesnuffer. But the front room were more of a cave an not so friendly. One little smoky stove bout nine inch across. Two skinny men on a little bench there suck up the feeble heat from that bad coal they use. Two doors an four windows in the one room an whats the good of em. Theys slapped together crooked an dont shut right. I close the door I come through an theys near enough room to crawl back out under it. Window curtains each a differnt bunch a stained an ragged patches. Ones blowin wet across the table got a greasy leg a mutton layin on it. Brush the flies an help yourself if you got your own knife says one a the men over his shoulder. He be friendly enough from whatever deep hole hes sunk in. Over to the corner who knows why but theres a harp slopped up in yellow paint. Slumped behind it is a man so drunk I didn even see him at first. Once in a while he pulls at the strings. Im there two hours fore I go upstairs to pull my boots off an all that time he mangle four damn slow chords over an over. *Zhing zang. Zhang zing.* Same four a anything for too longll put your mind in disarray. Grimy plaster bust a Sir Isaac on the mantle. Fancy sayins painted round the high moldings is done in them black dagger letters an somehow at odds with your general decrepitude. Take me a while to cipher out one beside the piss closet while Im waitin for a fellow to chuck up an slink back to his mugs. Somethin like this.

> *Subtle vortices of matter*
> *Made Sir Newton mad as a hatter*
> *Conjunction with projectile force*
> *Only made mad hatters worse*

Somehow it go along fine with our misty harpist on that drizzlin eve. *Zing zhang. Zang zhing.* I can hear him even now. Newtons not a place I frequent. Withy an the other factory masters here an yon stop from time to time as a natural meetin point. Center a their orbits you might say. An when Withy an his comperes start goin to the place it get fixed up fast. Nowadays its nicer than the Lion. Yet somethins wrong there.

I was there on one a them Saturdays feel like everbody cept me got his hand in someone elses pocket. Party a seven journeyman bakers barge in as if they own the place. Foul hearted an full breasted they command the area round the grate by means a their shameless drunk vulgarity an beshit like visages leerin everwhere. One a their swaggerin number they call Bovie. He jump up on a table an call out a wager. Says for a German dollar he will kill an eat a puppy dog one month old whats sleepin in a basket by the fire. The poor little thing was straight away grabbed from his brothers an sisters an handed by the baggy skin a his neck to this Bovie on the table top to a lewd cheer from the throng. I have just a glimpse a the little things tongue hangin out an his eyes strugglin to open. Bodies crowd in tight an the smell go bad in there. I hate to say it but it aint just them bakers. It be some a the regular Newton folk as well is cheerin him on. But even us folk as feel our throats choke up dont do nothin but not watch. So Bovie cut the squealin puppys throat then flay an put him on a grid iron an broil an eat him. An he was paid a dollar by a friend a his who was as proud as if he had won instead a lose the wager. Id say it take that Bovie twenty minutes to glut his black appetite. An the crowd growed rumblin quiet durin this time. A lady did retch an cry by the door but not one of us lift a knife to stop this damn bluebeard an thats the truth. I dont know why. Bothers me to this day. Like theres a gravitation there wont let you think a what youd do if you could move. I stay back an dint look close. But I didn leave neither. Leavin would be just as wrong. For that would be sayin do what you will while my back is turned. Somethin froze us all that night. Them slimy smilin bakers faces is like a dire pact you cant pry into or undo. But what you witness therell stick to you forever.

That wernt all. This Bovie stand up again an yell that for one dollar more he will eat the skin. If he did or no I cant say for as the mob is bubblin even darker in their coal smoked lusts some of us slink out by the side door. Cant take no more. Creepin by the bust a Sir Isaac Newton perched on the mantle I wonder at such a vile debauch before his stone blind gaze. Good thing Sir Isaacs stone ears is hid under his stone wig. You cant read nothin in that face. Its known Sir Isaac took no wife nor had a taste for maid servants nor plough boys nor pupils either way. All his time he calculates in private every numbered motion you can find. Give him seven eternities he couldn calculate you why a damned Bovie will kill an eat a puppy dog. And if this killin puppies is what a free man do then it may be that we should all be machines. Bolt mens arms to pulleys.

Strap their feet to treadles. Tie their fingers to the jack wires. Make em think a nothin but endless yards a cloth pilin up for someones profit. But linked to them machines they wont bloody that cloth with knives that gutted the yelp a some lost innocent. May be the only way we find gods grace is through gods machines. Im stabbed forever in my hearts ear by that puppys last yowl. Cant breathe right while Im walkin to my cart. My feets are wobblin an they pull me round behind the Newton. My thoughts is circlin behind themselves as well. Come back on the other side I see them seven bakers tumble out the door in their drunken blood flamed dither. They shout an huddle an each try to place one hand upon a stack a the others for a oath but couldn ever keep seven together cause some of em was always fallin backwards.

This is the part I never talk about before. I aint ashamed a what I done but then again I am. One day the one an one day the other. Thats the ways things be in life. They split up two an three an two an walk off in differnt directions. At Westhoughton Pike one of em turn right an then theres Bovie all alone on Macclesfield Road whistlin an belchin in a ugly combination. I wait till hes well along then I step quiet along the edge a the road some ways behind. I got no thought a what I tend to do though I do note I got a big sharp rock nestin on my shoulder. Now Im stridin in the open to catch up to him. Then Im runnin. Though its more a sidewise stumble carryin that stone. I calls out Bovie loud an clear. He turn round wobblin an his red face is all puffed an collapsed at the same time. We gots to look into each others eyes for it to mean anything but youd swear he couldn see a oak tree two feet away. For my part I dont even want the barest glimpse a him to stamp my vision. I says to him you killt that puppy for a hangin dollar. His face screw up into a question an I can see he already forgot the thing though bloods still smeared acrost his chin. I walk right up an says a dollar for that puppy dog but I do this for naught. I push that stone up over my head an just like Newtons ever droppin apple the gravitation in it pull me forward in a arc. Right before it smash into Bovies head I fix my eye on his. I see somethin blocked off in there. Somethin hid. Not like Great Mams cloudy sheep. Not like Newtons stony gaze neither. Hid from Bovie as well as me. But I know he seed where he was goin as the stone came down upon his weasly crouch. Dark brown spark a his understandin jump out at me in that one fateful instant. Then hes good an dropped there on the road side with his head punched in an blood runnin all round the pointed end a the stone an drippin on to the ground. I dont remember doin it. Aint never told about it till now. I almost feel like it happen with me or without me. Im just turnin through the gearlike motions a the turnin world.

HOW DO IT WORK

How do it work. How do it all go. It go by machinery. *Machine. Machination. Mechanical.* It operate by power spinnin the shaft. It run on steam. On steam collected in another place an brung here by pressure. Pistons. One thing move another. Marble hit a marble. Cept for Newtons apple. Cept for the moon. No one know who set them movin or why. I aint sayin I didn kill him. I turned away an left him flat an that be killin sure an dur.

Any way Bovies body get drug off before mornin. Not a word is spoke about any of it after that. Aint no one talk about him no more. Like he never was. Just that nameless rock still there beside the road. Still with a trace a red along the edge last time I look. Tiny squib in the *Notifier* a few days after. *Atrocious News.* It give no names but have a mention a the puppy dog. His names Ralegh. Didn have a name while hes alive. Just a puppy in a basket full a puppies an you tell the truth he might a end up drowned. But they call him Ralegh to remember him after he was killt an eaten. Thats good I think. Though truth is I aint heard Raleghs name for years neither. Ever thing is soon forgot. I keep that tore off piece from the *Notifier* for a while. It were the first issue a the paper printed on the new steam press. Ink get smeared an the paper get scored with the little grab marks. On the back side it say Fitzwell and Madsen. Hobble Town Road. Pure analeptic lemon acid. Families taverns and doctors will find it extremely convenient for bilious an similar disorders a the stomach an bowels. Contrived by the inventors as a remedy for ship captains. Dry an portable. To be had from druggists and confectioners. How can such two things be on one piece a paper. In the end I thow it in the hopper at the coal house an watch it go an fuel the general horse power. Like a tiny hair a Raleghs tail get twined into a piece a lace. A tiny word puff out the smoke stack an into the sky away. Maybe Johnny Dalton can tell me which atom. So thats when I killt a man. Not in Iron Boy wrangles like I expect. But this vile Bovie who come out a some dark nowhere an go back to that place. There wernt no good come out a that night. But you gots to wonder. Could be that sallow numberin gent hunched over in the hut done more harm than Bovie though not through blood lust. Fact he was your bloodless sort. An I didn kill him. Well aint no way on but onward.

Its when George Withy start to mount the guard round the manufactory durin the day we know the Iron Boysll be movin on it soon. One day when folk is gettin restive I hear Withy arguin with the mayor in the market stalls. Were a man whom I know to be honest an opulent an with whom I live in intimate friendship Withy says. Were such a man to come into my house where my wife Jane keeps the clock chains pulled an I have a footman who circulates with my portable table you might say to me rest in gods good graces for assuredly your friend will not stab you in order to rob you of your silver as it passeth him by. An I no more would suspect such an offense he says than I do an attack upon my manufactory. Which is solidly founded according to ancient rules an doth provide the Black Books honest day of work for every bootblacks whelp who wish it. No one can gainsay that. But. An here Withy raise a high finger like a fiery prophet. But this gentle friend of mine he may nonetheless be taken by a sudden unknown frenzy he says. Well not a one a us who hear this think Withy got a so called friend who would visit his home on any mission other than factory dealins. This sudden unknown frenzy Withy fear can only be one thing an that aint a friend stealin his silver from his portable table. It be us.

Enoch Taylor hes a iron founder. Wernt from round here but a good man none the less. He get charged with makin an repairin all the six inch frame wedges an twelve pound mounts an rocker arms an springs and shafts an other stuff for Withy. Course that do anger the men round this town who want the same work. But Enoch he also make sledge hammers on the side. An in a fit a pride to match his bulgin arms he make hammers biggern any one before. Great

Enochs theys called. You cant lift them things. People come from all over. Stoutest handles wont last on em. Six hunnerd good blows an you got to replant em. But they do the job. He make em with a skullsplitter ridge along the fore edge. He make em with a grabbin pike angled off to the back. Anything you want. I seen a Great Enoch crush a stood up twelve pound brick to red powder in one blow. That earn your respect. But a course it take a Great Enoch of a man to wield em. Aint got any a them amongst the Iron Boys so far twisted in so we stock up on Half Enochs an Little Enochs an even order up Baby Enochs for the ladies. Keep our Iron Boy armory inside Enochs foundry. Aint a better place to hide it in plain sight. Hammers an axes an swords an rifles. Pikes an sapper slings an even sacks a stones. Most of it be enough like Enochs work to raise no nosy eyeballs.

The days a comin. Everbody know it. An when it do come it feel like a day the teacher ask you to name all the kings. You know you can do it but may hap you cant. Ten a us Iron Boy numbers draw the eastern flank. Tam Brigby. John Gwilt. Sarah Maldon. Desmond Carke an me an Rose Stonewarden. An theres three other men an a lady who join up with us later accordin to the plan. Cant plan the weather a course. But the rain finally stop just at the right time for Desmond Carke to walk over to Six Acres to get the last instruction an the passwords. Would a took his horse but Pank says no. Too many people know about a horse. From what happen though he should a took a horse. Hes comin back by Priory Road past the side gate to Withys place. One a the dragoons in town his name is Wymondham. I know who he is from dancin days at the pavilion over to Dangington. Wymondham he stand there in the road out front a Withys gate like to say I dont even see you but Ill kick your arse an stomp you in the dirt just fine except for my new boots so I have my man do it for me. An that mump face John Norwood is smilin next to him an holdin Wymondhams bag. An Zepha Hames is standin cross the street by the long ditch with his arms folded but his right hand is on the silver knob a his knockin stick. So Carke come down the road with his hat slouched on his head like he always do. Wymondham he step out just enough to make Carke look round at the men there lookin at him. Wymondham says to Carke he says cover thy head. Carke says I shall do it for thee sir in simple faith as you have showed me no authority. So spite a Desmonds head already bein covered he take his hat off an then put it on again. Tuggin all round the edges bein careful not to tip it to the fellow. Aint like him to obey so quick someone he dont know. But its three over one an things is differnt on the road that night. He gots a mission not to be distracted from is how he tell it later. So Desmond get past him three four strides. Wymondhams daggers handed to him by John Norwood under cover of a basket cloth an he shout out. Authority. Authority is it thou wantest you knave. Authority I shall give thee then. Suchlike regal words dont match his raw yelpin but I guess hes tryin to bump up his menace. Whats left to do but Desmond turn round an draw his own dagger an run an poke at Wymondham an Wymondham slice back at him. Desmond get his knuckles cut an flee down the alley on the other side a the long ditch an round the corner into the back way to Rose Stonewardens place where he was supposed to end up anyhow.

Wymondham an Zepha Hames go round by the street side an cast stones at Roses big oak door there. Then together they come up an heave a stone bigger than a farthing loaf through the window where it crash an thunk down on the floor an rock back an forth in front a the china cabinet an make the teacups clink. Then Norwood run in the front door an Mildreds little Janie is screamin from that stone crashin down right next to her two rag dollies sittin up talkin to each other at a tiny table. Aint no doubt Norwoods paunchy face scare her too as well it should. Rose pull Janie by the hand up the back stairs an says come up quick. Your dolliesll protect us. Norwood he go out the door again after thowin a heavy nut pick at the two of em on the stairs. Desmond hes under the kitchen table drippin blood from his knuckles but he trail Norwood back to Withys gate screamin at him. Wymondham call Desmond a fart bag an a foamin dog. Carke says back to him youre a pissin toad who aint worth the effort a crushin your skull for the toad stone. Then he stomp an turn an call Zepha Hames green squirrel shit an John Norwood a damn bog sucker. Come by yourself or send the best man you got an Ill answer you one for one. All this despite Desmond knowin theres more important business that night. Which make you wonder why it all happen right next to Withys house. Hames he run into Withys garden shed to fetch a spear an sword an he thow Wymondham the sword. Right then is when I come along on my cart supposed to pick up Desmond an the others. Cart wernt the same no more cause Gladden that poor old thing she go off to the knackers yard not long before. She knowd it was comin when she fall down one day right off her legs. An when we push her back up she wernt goin anywhere no more. Just stood there stuck lookin all wild eyed an sinkin down again an again. All she do is nibble my sugared fingers once for a sweet good bye. Wouldn look at me. I didn blame her then. But I wish now Id had that last look in her eye.

I dont know if I tell you but after Brindles move off an leave Oatsy an Muslin behind at the bake house I take them two horse over to Mechanick Arts. I mean what else can I do. At least I figure they be fed good there cause they can work. Unlike the mice an toads in that place who just gets fed an killt as fars I know. So when Gladden she go down I ast em if I can have one a the two of em back. They tell me Oatsys the one. Muslins more the eager horse so he get all the attention an the experiments on him. I think he may even a done some a the horse power calculations. Could be hes a famous horse if any one knowd about it. I like Oatsy but he aint Gladden. Shorter legs an his attention wander from the road. So Rose shes prayin loud in the alley an peekin down the long ditch. I dont know nothin yet but I says Rose take Desmond back inside with you an wrap his hand an sling it up. Wymondham he shout out that Rose is a strong legged whore an he would like to see her prance after worship. Carke he wont be tended even by Rose but go an stand in the street in front a her place suckin the blood off his knuckles. Zepha Hames follow him there with a two handed sword which he swing wild with before Wymondham call out for him from somewhere. Zepha an them drift off shoutin vile language back over their shoulders. An Withy hes never to be seen nor even his ostlers or gate men through all a this.

So there we was sittin in the cumber room in the back a the Newton. Tam Brigby. John Gwilt. Sarah Maldon. Desmond Carke. Myself. Rose Stonewarden. We be the east flank a the proposed attack. Pank House decide that. The oath. The twistin in. The magnetism an the Iron Seed. All that nows the path what lead us to this damp room where we be tucked down over our mugs watchin the walls darken an brighten an darken again while it rain the whole long afternoon. Your vasty kind a drops swingin back an forth. Out the window nothin but a raw flat stretch a treeless ground an clouded sky. Cloud wraiths is sailin to the west. Pond out back which you think must overflow but dont. White birds from the sea shore flatten themselves down betwixt the raw mole hills then flutter up an flatten down again elsewhere like some kind a game. Puddle a rain trickle under the back door. I just watch it crawl an stop an pool an crawl an that be my occupation. Servin girl come in to swab the floor an top us off. How much difference between your mop an this slop Tam says with his fingers pinch together like no difference. Little kiss from Molly here would even it up he says. This enough for her to stop an smile an wring out her mop on his boots. After a while the sky whites up to a stray sun beam an the grasses fatten in the steamin dew an the eave drips in separate drops. Then the dark pourin cataract come down again. Nothin to do but sip that hoppy ale.

Pank come in an stalk around an fling his wet silence all about. Eyes us each one by one. We dont eye him back. As was instructed. He was testin us. We eye each other instead. Pank put his flat shiny hand over top a Carkes mug as if to say enough. Then he stare out the back window for a time. I can hear the numbers tumblin in his head. *This aint like the time when two bobbin boys cut six jack wires to stop three frames for four dang days* he want to say but cant. Things is fast an big now. Numbers is swellin. Attack tonight is supposed to be two hundred souls or even more.

Come at Withys from all four sides. Four waves on each side. Plans was drawed up in colored lines on a big sheet a paper. First wave be musket men to engage the militia whats posted night an day now ten yards out. Second wave pistols an swords close quarter at the gate posts to divert the guards. Third wave axe men to chop open the doors an windows. Fourth wave is us smashers with our hammers an apples. I dint feel good about it. Almost couldn get myself to dress that morn. Then Pank make the quick sign an thow up his hood. Bell the rat to scare the cat he says an walk off into his silver gloom. Molly come in again. She wipe the tables an wander round for somethin else to do. We aint even at the gamin boards so she go out an in an out again. Day like this feel like we all be just sweepin up our own broom straws. Afternoon as long as a week a afternoons. Gwilt get up an go to the window. Them thick brows hang over his eyes like little caves hes peerin out of. Then Carke haul hisself up with his thumbs in his pockets. He leave the room despite the firm instruction. No one put a glance to it though. Time be movin so slow Carke could ride off to Runny Pumps an back an no one swear he even been gone.

Light begin to fade again. You listen close or may be far away the drip an tinkle a the rain in all its little places is growin like music while you didn notice. Damn sight better than that *zing zhang* harp that day at the Newton. Then I think I hear a bird plaint in the midst. My ears prick up cause birds dont sing in the rain. May hap theys heard a our plans. May be they know somethin. May be they start talkin to me again. When its too late. Then by the muffle an the graspin scrapin rhythm I knowd Carke was pressin his pleasure upon maid Molly somewhere on the floor boards above. Pleasure an emptiness an rain an beer weigh heavy on me. I look at Sarah but she darn away her thoughts there with the needle workin. Some while later Carke come back. His feet is clumpin but his face is clear. Desmonds one of em whos always tellin you how many times he bedded down a wench. How many times with Mary Louise. How many times last week. He sure to tell you he have three wenches in one day one time an the most times he did one wench in one day is six. If one be good why do three or six matter I ast him once. Sometimes a thing dont itch till you scratch it he says to me. That like to be true for all a us those days.

They say five it aint so good in itself but worketh well in combination. I think thats true. Now I be fifty an some annos. Thats a number way beyond the last square number I seed in this life an way before the next. So Im dependin now on five in all its combinations. None a my numbers so far is my Iron Boy number though. I aint reached that yet. Afternoons as a lad I use to lie with my nose in the grass an watch all them teeny speck bugs movin along underneath. Each stalk an blade got its own shadow an protection for that world tween my eyes an my cheeks. You wonder is there someone watchin us like Ise watchin them bugs an they not knowin of it. Bout the time I reach my last square number I start feelin old. You fiddle with John Peter he mostly just belly over an dribble out. Aint so sweet a spark as in the golden days a Silvys French moss rubbin up an down my leg an her tryin to love me as good as she can. Which she done as good as anyone. Then the smashins come an that keep me goin. An wonderin whatll happen. Day after day. But riddle me this. Is night an day a wheel. Is they a machine. Which way do it turn. Which way is we goin. Runnin towards the dawn or leapin into night. Some times you gots to wonder.

This is the thing. Ever time I come to tellin about the smashin a Withys I dont want to get into it. Why is that. Years go on you find it hard to think you was young once an had hard spit on the back a your tongue an hear the birds an know the words an why the veins a iron jump out a the earth an what the stubble fields winnow from the breeze. Two ways I can see for a story to stay hid. Ones obfuscation like the dang birds whose mission may not even be so clear as pure deception. Chirpin half a versicle you may not understand at first or ever. May they tweet in hell them kind a birds. Black Book be like that. Sometimes I want to call it the Black Bird Book for that reason. All the verse got numbers in that book. Second King. Twenty five an eight. *An in the fifth month on the seventh day a the month which is the nineteenth year*

HOW DO IT WORK 211

a King Nebuchadnezzar king a Babylon come Nebuzaradan captain a the guard a servant a the king of Babylon unto Jerusalem. And he burnt the house a the lord and the kings house an all the houses a Jerusalem an every great mans house burnt he with fire. Theys even a whole book called Numbers in there. *By their generations. After their families. By the house of their fathers. According to the number of the names. From twenty years old and upward. All that were able to go forth to war. Those that were numbered of them were fifty and four thousand and four hundred. And they shall set forth in the second rank.* Could be us theys talkin about in there. Verily verily I say unto you one thousand six hundred an sixty six times gods grace is lace. I suppose in the Black Book theyre tryin to convey the word inside the word. Cept all them words is trapped in numbers.

The other way a tale stay hid is Corbels way. Tellin no one nothin until now. But it be so many bark boats under the bridge you dont know what get forgot an what get lost amid the clang a everthing what come crowdin after it. What wont never now be told. What Im tired ofs all thats loose an chancy on the tongues in the blabber lappin at the Green Lion or the Newton or wherever men drink an piss. All thats told so much that no one pay attention no more. Even when its true. Like the *Notifier.* You dont know what be important in the end. It could be the stockin dance or that pig race at Fool Fair. Might be our twistin in or the fright a Nancys face. Or the Iron Seed an horseshoe business. Or the number man in the cheese hut. Or Eddard Weedys telescope or the comet wine. Or Widow Dedorays weepin or Ben Maldons music master brung from France for Colin or what not all wove in. Who know whatll linger. What signify. What the childrens children tell their children. Whatll last. Like Forty Fours proud monument. Be it only cheap wood chiseled an charcoaled up to look like stone but anyhow not just made a smoke. That I reckon is the point a me tellin you all this.

One by two we squeeze through the back door a the fallin down ruin what was the old granary before they move the pond. No moon. Pank House change his tune I guess from the twistin. Granarys just across the old mill race ditch from the manufactory shippin yard. Where all the tracks go in so it aint the easiest place to guard. Too cold to be a proper night on which to black your face an puff up your wig. Coal dust an lamp powder wont stick at all or else they blotch up in the goose grease. Those with smilin or frownin masks an dyed horse hair to stick to their necks or those with cowls an high collars is better off. But we do it one way an another. Cept for me. Im goin in to collect the order numbers an shippin bills for tomorrows run as usual an meantime have a look around inside. That were the notion any road. It dont happen that way. Sarah an one a the new men they amplify their disguises smilin at each other with extra twists a straw stuffed in like corn maids even though

John say dont do it cause you wont move as good. First time I seen Sarah smile in two months. Rose even come out with a box a fox tails. Where from I dont know but we all attach em somewhere like our little sign amongst us. The fox tail flank. Sarah tub up her long black slender hair under a beetle hat she keep from a play she was in once. I wisht I knew what her name was in it cause when she slide that hat down an shove her fingers up to tuck under her hair an start steppin out her legs wide an straight I know shes actin an I want think Im in the play with her. A little world where we could be together an others see us but dont see us if you know what I mean. From up top a the beam in the granary you can look out the old vent holes. Eight or ten a what seem kings riflemen cause a their gold epaulets is amblin along around the factory walls stabbin scraps with bayonets an pickin up pebbles as if theys bullets an eyeballin back an forth. In between em the irregulars look more like children about to be whipped than proper pikemen defendin a line. Theys armed with long handled axes an big hammers though not Enochs since they dont know about his. I can see two men crouchin on the roof behind the W in Withys sign. I think I make out a steamin cauldron up there an what look like four pocket cannons restin on the parapet.

Group a rowdy Child Town lads over on our western flank is makin some kind a provocation in nice drill order.

Thow ten apples
At the top
Soon that top
Is gonna drop

A line a ten or so of em I reckon. Though I can see some girls clappin an kickin an rhymin in between. They been in trainin. Any one can see that. But who put em to it is the question. The boys lean back an fling some a them small red November Charms hard up at the men on the roof. Only thing is you got to know which apples be which. Little round blister a yellow paper stuck on the apple cheek. That be the Iron Boy signature. Tiny dot a hoof glue keep it put. No harm if you eat it. Basket a Iron Boy apples get to market by mistake once. I see the poor fellow tryin to peel back them labels. Pulls a patch a skin right off a every one. He thows them dang things hard away disgusted. So you get the sayin. *Cant make a apple change its spot.* Good arms them Child Town lads is got. Fast. One hit one a them rooftop men on the shin an he have to dodge an slump down on his arse up there.

Apple hit you
On the leg
You are gonna
Have to beg

Then come another barrage so swift an smooth they must a put some serious drill into it.

Apple bonk you
On the head
You are gonna
Drop down dead

Second man swerve an slip an stick his foot into that cauldron which look to be full a hot tar an hes screamin an writhin about up there. Cauldron tip over an the rest a the tar run down the side a the buildin till it cool on the bricks. Good thing too. Guns an skullcrack podgers swung by newt brained oafs we can handle but not black pitch rainin from above.

Some folk is marchin not with the Iron Boys an not under Ludds banner neither. Dont know who they be but they has a differnt sort a song. Each a their little band got a sword or a slingin sack with a big stone in it or a sharp stake or a grabbin iron. Whatever it is theys swingin with precision. One got nothin but a broom stick. Down an cross an up an back an flip it with a shout an start singin again. You almost want to think theys doin it not for the mill smashin but for the lusty hell of it.

Do your crank hang low
Do it wobble to an fro
Can you tie it in a knot
Will you tie it in a bow
Do you thow it on your shoulder
Like a continental soldier

Do your crank
Hang
Low

Then a quick turn on their toes an theys marchin back the other way right up tight with each other. I aint never seed the like an I never do find out who they is.

Do your shank aim high
Do it reach up in the sky
Do you pump it full a spunk
So it shoot into your eye
Do you shove it in your holster
Like a continental soldier
Do your shank
Aim
High

John Gwilt he get such a tickle it wont let his stomach go an he have a hard time keepin his beard on straight. What I cant believe is the manufactory is still runnin amidst all this though not full force. Stacks is smokin an gears is turnin an one two carts is still trottin off from the finishin shed under guard. Just not so frequent. Though I see one so called guard up side down drunk about to drop off the back a the cart an another pickin his finger nails with a apple knife. Pank say spies is plaitin themselves in everwhere. Which is one reason we Iron Boys pull away from Luddish arrangements.

HOW DO IT WORK 217

Early on they was a conversation tween Timothy Twist an Truck Merriman. This is way back at the beginnin. Long before them first Ned Ludd oaths. Front an center table at the Cat an Spyglass. Merriman he was coachman to a lady who was writin falsehoods for the *Notifier* an them Big Town magazines about Ludds men an the smashins all about. She come through here once. Wide brim hat. Seven bracelets on her writin arm. Why would you do that. Miss Bliss I think is her name in the papers. You couldn not like her some. Kind a perfume make you want to heave a sigh to get more in you an remember it when shes gone. She dont smile at anyone though. Earnest lady. Dont know why folk is so eager to look at all that black print. Get to the bottom an turn the page an think cause you see them words all lined up tidy you know somethin at the end of a sentence. I stop readin somehow after I lose my legs. Could be your feet is connected to your eyes. Eyes are feet pokin in the air. Feet is eyes lookin through the earth. Both of em move you about. But Truck Merriman I seed him around later without Miss Bliss an ploppin down money like you know he aint required to be no coachman. Sharin this table with Timothy Twist at the Spyglass like I say. Players on a stage an just that loud. They want you to hear em. That Twist. He were a velvet maze. Mister Twisty. Once I call him that. Nothin but a slight turn an a light smile. *Sir* Twisty for your souls sake he says. You have to like the general ornacy of his speechifyin. Listenin to hims like slidin down a spiral banister. Sir Twist spread his arms like a bird dryin hisself. Ludd. Ludd. Only this morning did it come to me. He is for us to decide. Half wit of Macclesfield. Perhaps. Perhaps. Whipped for shirking an come back to smash. Good. Who would not believe it. My dear Merriman he says. So much must be clear to all who incline in our direction. Let us hide our spark in his cloak of ill used flesh. Let us give him our dark lantern for his dark places. Let him be legend. Let us hear of General Ludd and King Ludd and even Mother Ludd. And we shall let the poor lad Ned Ludd upturn the apple cart and seize the magic pippin. Snip off the princes golden beard and trade it for a bag of salt. Fling factory folk to the wolves below Tit Peak. Pour bees wax over the iron thorns choking the stream. Perhaps a song or two about him would be good. Truck glump down the local suds. Twist sip his canary wine. Thinkin. Then he come up with this in a musical voice.

I hide myself in a shaving bowl
A sack of nails will buy my soul
And when years end brings on a sigh
Youll find me in your Christmas pie

I know what you want to ask Twist says. Dare we duff him up in so much puffery. Yes I say and Ill tell you why. Like that smoke from your pipe each story will rise and dissipate yet leave a strong scent in the air. And as our story changes so he changes. And as our story gallops off he simply disappears.

We make him come
We make him go
He is our lad
We like him so

Come come my merry man. Let us cogitate together. But Merriman he just sit there pattin his paunch an preenin his gumps. *Jahar jahar jahar.* He got that sort a laugh. Believe what we tell em he says back to Twist. Smoke dont twist for nothin he says fist on the table. You got that right he says watchin his fingers pick his nose. Truck Merriman. Cant say why I dont like him but I dont. Dont know what those two be doin together neither. Twist gyre his empty glass so it wobble across the table with a *rowr rowr rowr* like that. Truck he grab out to stop it at the edge but the sudden motion tip his fat arse off the chair an onto the floor where he belong. Ise glad to see it but I wish itd been at the Newton so that blind bust above the door could laugh inside at such a rumpy demonstration of his apple law. At that very moment Sir Twisty twist around to look me smack in the eye. Like he just took a castle with a horse an dare me to see whats comin next. One look thats it. Then he turn back an clap Truck on the shoulder an hardy dardy they take their leave from each other like fine old folk. Then you aint sure what you hear an see no more. You know how it go in a ale house. Most of its chuffin your own feathers an spittin swill at the other man. But I couldn get that look out a my head.

Are you gonna blink on me is what it says. I try an think of everwhere I ever seed him. Put it all together cause he may be the dancin cat holdin the spyglass like on the sign out front. An does Twist got anything to do with our twistin in. But you cant never get to the bottom of it all.

Wernt long after Twists dramatic postulation you do start to hear tales a Ned Ludd here an there an his army an such. Sharp an close to hand. People say they see the fellow. Like the young fellow who curl up most a that winter inside the manufactory. Back part a the boiler house. I seed him asleep in a old coal scuttle Miss Eveline Fray the book keeper had filled with lace spoilage from when they was shuntin out cart loads a bad loops. Lad sleep most a the day ans out all night like a cat. Never say a word to no one. Sleepy eyes an maybe aint learn how to talk. Ever one knowd hes there though. Youd poke a foot in his ribs to rouse him when the floor master come by. Miss Fray who work in Withys office she would come out an scrub his howlin face once a week with that stangin soap an water they use to clean the grease an thread dust off the needles. Dish a old bread mashed up with thin milk if the dogs dont get it. But watch out. This lad would scratch you. One mornin he was spied an marched down the back stairs among the rest an chained to a disused stockin frame in the corner. Down where the lights weak an nobody much is watchin you. He dint have to do nothin.

Up above they stop at sundown. Hes forgotten an chained all night. Next morn his frame an two mores been nullifed by bashin em with a brick. His chains is broke an no one seed him since. For some weeks Im thinkin that lad fit the story a Ned Ludd. So you might believe it all. Upturn the apple cart an seize the magic pippin. Bees wax over the iron thorns. Thats how a story nag an snag you. How can you tell who spin the thread an who write this.

> *I am King Ludd*
> *I wear no crown*
> *The ladies laugh*
> *When I fall down*
> *You ask my name*
> *I beg you pray*
> *Whats made of iron*
> *Yet blows away*

Each one got his own view a everthing now. Many folk Pank says may be carryin torches to fire factories same as we be doin. But now each got his own reason. Pank tryin not to move his lips tell me there be reason even Withy may want to burn his own manufactory. This aint somethin I can put together in my mind. Then Pank says to me so theys a fellow come smilin at you with a knife between his teeth. Which come first Corbel. The smile or the knife. Teeth come first I says an I know I has him. Thats good. Ill remember that he says.

So Im there that fateful night in the factory collectin the orders an bills an lookin around an I ask but they tell me Withy aint been seen that whole day anywheres about. Which is a odd thing on this of all days. I walk into his office with the papers to get the signatures for the night deliveries. Eveline Fray shes half sittin behind the desk like she got a tack on her seat. Mister Penner what do I do she whisper without lookin at me. First time she ever talk to me by name. I tell her she should get her a ladies ache if she got some place to go to. An may hap she did cause no one see her after that day. Hung on the wall there I see the big rule boards been added to since the week before.

Any sick with loud complaint no cause visible – six pence

I see another thing as well. Guards has been put in the places a some a those who dont come in to work. They got weapons to hand one sort or another. An three four pyramids a rifles is butted up here an there. Miss Fray sign Withys name just like Withy hisself to each one a my pages in the clip. I go back out I see a row a cannon balls lined up down the long hall but I dont see no real cannon. Them pocket cannons on the roof just shoot stones. All your daytime plannin dont seem worth much when night come down. We has our sacks a apples an ample iron stuff. Fourth rank on the east flank. All numbered off. China crackers an roman candles an firework stars go up an come down over us. Green blue white an fat red bangs. You cant tell who set em off or whether theys to signal or distract us or them with all that bright smoke an noise an curly wurly. Or to light up the battle which come on a sudden. First ranks a rifle men advance. Shoot out some windows an raise some brick dust an flyin shards. The intention is to peel em back not kill em. After the rifles come the second rank. They aim to shunt the guards off the gates with close quarter pistols an swords. Threaded in amongst em is some Child Town lasses we know aint gonna be shot at. Who would shoot Sally Child Town. A course later on that do happen but you never would think it then. An the Child Town lads is good at roamin round an askin for tobacco an sweets an notin the movements a men an guns an such. I even see Milky slip his way past the guards an disappear inside. A nod an a wink later hes on the roof top talkin with them two up there. He wander round an point down at us like a half captain plannin maneuvers. First to the west side then to the south. Then over to me an Sarah Maldon like hes one a them. He get em marchin around up there so I can see there be four not two. Ise proud a that lad. I wouldn a done nothin like that or even thought of it when Ise his age. Then Milky pull out a white cord an tie it round the big *C* in the *Co* an slide down. Nimble feet kickin off the bricks. Hair pokin ever which way as it flop in an out a the lights. I dont see him when he hit the ground so I dont know whether he gots one a them new pocket lucifers what you scratch on a brick to fling up a flame or he go borrow a torch from some one but next thing is that white cord is splutterin white sparks an burnin. Its near sparked itself to the top a the wall before I know its a fuse. I call to the front lines to get back quick cause somethins goin to blow.

What it is is the clock. First its sittin up there like always with them arrows pointin to your *Ix* an your *Vi* or what not an then its gone in a big bang an a puff a smoke an crackin wood an clankin gears an wrenched metal squeakin horrible like when two men jerk tenpenny nails out of a thick board with a claw hammer. An X come off the dial an clip one a Withys guards bad in the shoulder. He lie there rollin on the ground an howlin. Nowdays you almost laugh to think a them numbers sprangin out an havin their way in the rough world instead a in the minds a men. Theys lucky them hands like swords didn go right through one of em. I mean it was numbers in the head is what convince George Withys countin men to save him money by makin the jack wire pinions with less metal. First they try to shave em off an melt down the shavins but thats too much work. So they send for a man to calculate the measure down to a exact hairs breadth less. Save a penny on a thousand of em. You an me we wouldn notice it or care. But for Withys men them calculations must give em little rubs a pleasure like strokin a cat. Trouble is them new pinions break more often an has to be replaced. But I guess Withy figure that in since he have his own pinion factory over to Little Glossop.

Any road Milky come back down an tell me theys another big cauldron a tar on the roof an where its hid so we can keep a watch. After the pistols an the axe men come the hammers an apples. Rose insist on swingin one a them Lady Enochs. I can tell she never do feel at home with thowin knobbly potatoes or Iron Boy apples. It just dont make sense to her. I can understand that. Along side Rose is Tam Brigby an John Gwilt ready to go. Tam despite his mask you always know him by them haystack muscles. Cant make a shirt sleeve to fit him without it lookin like a clown puff. The whole line is swingin Enochs which is so new they show bright flashes in the torch light. Theys all ready to romp an we apple throwin Iron Boys lurk behind em for the final blows. Lalloways weavin in an out somewhere with her big feet on tiptoes holdin New Billy by the hand who got a damp patch on his trouser front. Fireworks bam an bloom in the sky an then one big crackin roar an screamin an shoutin *hey hey hey hey heyyyyy ohhhhh* rise up all around. An there we go. In the back rank we can hear the crashin windows an metal clankin inside. You hear a dozen tales about where the first spark come from. But when we see the flames its no mistake an time to do it.

You wouldn believe the purgatory there already when I get inside. Lookin back on it now I can see it like I couldn see it then. Metal an wood an wires an threads an cloth is lyin in a huge mess. The airs still thick with shards an dust. Its upsettin no mistake to see such disorder in the factory. Even though its the *pilchin fuckin twankin* a the damn factory as Tam Brigby put it is what do pound each a us into such disorder bettern the biggest Enoch. Pound us so soft an hard that we forget what all it done to us. Just like we forget Old Sheppey an what it done to him. You almost hear a screamin from the smokin piles. They was some rifle shots goin each way but most a the fightins hand to hand. An there aint much of it in the end cause them big Enochs has their way. Then the flames is leapin more than lickin. All that light an smoke you cant see much. Wes each supposed to find a target. You know it when you see it. I cant tell you more than that Pank says. But when a brick wall collapse in front a you you dont know what youre seein. You just know you in a hurry. You dont got time to know what others is doin. Flamin factory beams is shrivelin to black ribs against the sky. I never feel such a heat. My face is burnin off for sure an the glowin metal in there aint like no fire I ever stoked. This be where souls could get melted down. You find out what you got left over for the devil. My legs is like flamin trunks rooted in the ground. What can this bleedin apple do to hells bright gates you wonder. But I heave that thing to disappear in the flames before it bake right in my hand.

Them charred beams is saggin like boilin treacle. Nothin smell right. I turn an run as goods I can through the flamin chunks an then I hear the wall. Thick brick wall come apart in the heat an just slump down on itself sendin out a rollin Black Wopper wave a choky dust an shards a mortar an the bones an trash an hard dung they stuff into the hollow of it when they first build it. Come down like it just melt into itself. Cant escape. Course I didn see it. I was in it. Its Milky tell me what it was like. Hes outside warnin folk about the tar on the roof an passin the word on what else he seed from up there. Then he come back in to look for me. Im tryin to run through ruin. That big wall its been held in place by the beams which is now burnt away. An that triangle arch made of brick up in the top corners. Them bricks is the ones dump down on me an smash my lower half. I dont remember nothin.

*In apples fall
we sinned all.*

They tell me its moren a week fore I wake up an know who I am. First I has to find out about my legs. There aint no nice bird sittin in my window to chortle quizzically I tell you. Factory smashin is still clangin in my head like a cracked gong bein beat by the likes a New Billy. Your mind wander wild an you see all things bright an gnarly on that black drop they give you to kill the pain. *Finest Extra Wide Fancy Ribbon.* That old sign where the letters they curl like ribbon. Plum red in front with the color a fiery moonrise on the back side where the letters fold over. Where could I a seen it. Withy dont make ribbon. But I can feel that soft plush ribbon with my fingers in the air floatin in my eyes sure an dur. An them lynxes snarlin at me from the moonlight. Tryin to pull my sheets off with their claws. I ask everbody who come in the room after I wake up what happen. No one seem to want to tell the story to me. Like they know somethin I aint ready to hear. Thats what I think at first when Im lyin there an cant move. Later I think its not me. Its somethin turn gray in their faces. Its a new way a not lookin at you. They just dont want to talk about it. Well cockles alive I want to talk about it. The whole thing. Ludds men. Did any body see Timothy Twist that day. Is Sarah fine. Where was Withy. What about the apples. Where is Pank. But all I get is Withys is burnt down to the ground. Later on someone tell me that the smashin go like a pig on ice. Im the only one get crushed when the roof fall in. I gots to say to myself over an over Im lyin in Lyington at the limb hospital. Lyin in Lyington at the limb hospital. Cause with the black drop you dont remember minute to minute. People in hospital theys a world apart. The skeleton in the corner laugh half the night keepin me awake so I start poundin the mattress an twistin my sheets till they drip. May be they dont got the same sense a the event over here. I mean its further away than Raw Morton though I know they was at least one Iron Boy from Lyington. That wall keep slumpin down on me like dream bricks. Pain makes my missin legs seem to get up an run. Everthings swirlin.

Even when I poke at nurses hangin debbies when she bend over me it dont feel real. Even when Im sayin to myself over an over Im lyin in Lyington at the limb hospital. Lyin in Lyington at the limb hospital.

Nurse give me a sponge bath once or twice but as Im dreamin away I remember Silvy shes the first one givin me a proper soak an scrubbin. I mean some one must a took a brush to me when Ise too young to know about it cause I remember stingin all over. Smack your head with the handle an scrub your bum with the bristles an that brush be like anger in a scratchy piece a log. Nancys mama have some anger in her brush as well. I can see that now. I never did no washin but what I scoop from a basin or a horse trough an splash it on an pat it round an rub it with a rag if I gots one to hand. Or dry out in a warm breeze in the summer time. Splash my face in the mornin to keep the gnomes from cruddin up my eyes so I dont stumble into their string traps. An my stinkin parts I find a way to fresh em up regular enough. You rub under your arms with a crushed sprig a sweet belly rue or mash a hand full a chidderly leafs around your dingle thatll do good enough for a week or so. Only thing I ever do to my feet though is pull em out a my boots at night an wave em in the air. I hire a lady once in a while to wash my shirts an foot bags an dependin on the lady my crotch bags if I dont thow em in the fire while I wrap up in a old blanket or robe she give me. Some times the ladyll give you a hot meal an even shave you. Thats the pinnacle. But that scrub in a tub from Silvy its a memory. An now Im livin it again.

Veuve she had a deep stone trough way back in the yard. Big eyed mooly faced what you call its lookin at you from the front end. Like them stone faced cherubs with the cheeks pissin for joy into fountains. These guys though has leafy branches comin out a their mouths an off a their eye brows. Any road Veuves tubs all slick inside with black mossy stuff. You sink down an you got a furry pad under your sittin bones. It tickle your crack an soothe your backside softern any high puff cushions you ever sat polite on. Water run in from the roof catchers an down the side a the barn. Silvy let me know Im gonna get washed good this time. I hear her sayin somethin I think its about love but turn out its French for washin. She thow some broke up hot bricks from the back a the oven down in the deep end. Big hiss give up a whush a steam. I settle my arse down. Water got a black cast from whatever it is is growin down there. Cant tell you how penetratin it is to settle down in that hot soup. Got to rise back up into the chill two three times fore I get use to it. My knees is two bare knobs pokin out like giant babys knees theys so bare an smooth. I never seen em like that. My legs look all small. Or may be magnified I dont remember but bent off crooked. Could be its a sort a water magnetism do that to em. Or was it a glimpse a the future right there in that water. Then Silvy pour in a big pot a steamy water she brung out from the kitchen. Her poky elbows is pushed together an her neck cords is strainin as she hold it up with a towel wrapped round the handle. As she tip it over that steamin cataract pour right on the fork of a mans nature. I do me a rump jump out the water an I get a stab like lightnin through my gristle. But then its a echo throb like thunder two hills over. Then it be just fine. But there be numbers roilin in that water. With my eyes closed I see two two nil two nine seventy four six fifty seventeen nine an five an six pourin over me. I can feel the little hooks on the nines an fives an sixes. Silvy she look serious an happy with her grin behind the swish a hair swingin cross her face as she bring out a small ivory fancy ladys brush an grab up my feet an with no sweet overture she start explorin a whole new land down there. Feels like a unknown valley an a hill an a ridge line round my walkin pads. Shut your eyes an you see better. Then she come to the toes an she could be stringin a pearly necklace. *Archipelago.* I dont know if that be the word but its what mumble up on my tongue. Im all unorient an upside down so I ope my eyes to get my bearin back. Silvy gots her own eyes closed. Look like some unholy prayer when she snake her tongue out slow an start to lick my feet. Foot pads is thick enough I dont feel it direct but more the pressure an the sight of it give me a wobble like I tumble into some Black Book tale. Whereby *my feet are sunk in mire but I put all my things square under em. A woman did wash em with her tears an wipe em with the hairs a her head an kiss my feet an make em like hinds feet an set me upon my high places.* Then she spread out my big toe an the next one an draw her long tongue fro an to between. I knowd her tongue is strong from when she slide it around my teeth an push my jaw around. An then she do between the next toe an the next an the next one an the next. I say good bye little piggy when she stop to suck on him a while. Then the other foot which by that time I forget I got. Her tongue between my toes is like my face down in her ladies place. Like openin doors that never been open. I watch her with her eyes closed when she pull a long wet strand a hair behind her ear an move her mouth right on up my leg. Bouncy water from the hangin branches steam an drip down all around us. When she get right up there my juice spurt out a me an curdle in the water like candlefish roe. It be a moment. I wont say no more. Only thing was Silvy scrub her smell off a me. The spot in the crook a my thumb where I can rest my nose an whiff up her fine furry stink any time after for most a week. Got to be careful not to snuff it moren once a day to make it last. Some tang in her down there aunt no one else like that. But then shes gone an its gone with her an with all that happen since I cant conjure anything about it no more. What I do recall the smell of is the soap she use to wash me that day. Oats to scrape you an butter milk to soothe you. Shaped like a little pear you can wrap your hand around. Never did bend my trail to search for another scrub like that. Man had his habits in those days. An without Silvy I didn care.

So it take a while before I get the wheels put on this seat contraption an get the coffin maker to put me on his wagon when he got a light load one day an take me back to town. I roll myself round an about the heaps a stone an metal in the black space where Withys was. Air still feel like its smokin though it aint. Factory field. Pig race. Cheese hut. The men who move the pond. One thing leadin to another. You try to measure the angle where the clock use to be. Where was the hat rack where all the wagerin went on over who could ring their cap first. Where was the countin table an the teasel beds. Withys window wall. That room I saw a man doin somethin he shouldn with some Child Town lass. Ise thinkin this be how a angel see. Right through all our buildins an doins like theys nothin there. They care about somethin else. Lot a folk come by to scuff a look or two without sayin much. I stay longer cause I aint used to gettin around on wheels yet. Grounds full a rubble and your arms get tired.

Pank stroll up slow with a pipe in his mouth. Like he always have a pipe though its something new. New things already crowdin out the old things. I didn know what to say to him. It wernt cause we dont want to talk about it. Im thinkin a all a those questions I just said. Ludds men. Is Sarah fine. Withy.

What did Iron Apples do. Timothy Twist. Somehow all we been through them questions dont ring true no more. Wouldn be any good answers now. Guess you wont be Lady Pank no more I says. Guess you wont be roamin roads no more he says. Things seem bigger now I says. Or may be Im smaller. You figure that one out Pank says you come an find me. Ill be around. Then he walk off kickin at brick ever once in a while.

They claim six dead but that was lyin testimony at the trial. Three militia may a got killt we dont know. They dont produce but the one body. So called Charlie Harley. Wailin about him as if we all knowd an loved him. No one knowd him an thats a fact. You hear folk singin a song to swoon the ladies an not just in the Cat an Spyglass neither. I hear it sung in the Green Lion where once theyd a laughed such a thing into a puddle a suds. I know he didn work at Withys. Theys tryin to create a martyr on the other side.

> *Charlie Harley was my darlie*
> *Dillie dapper an far faring*
> *Was my daring dear*
> *Charlie Harley had me nearly*
> *Never will I find another*
> *For my lover here*

Someone make it up after the smashin. As if it be a old song. It aint a old song. All we know they could a brung any old strangers carcass out from

Westhoughton ice house an stab it like that an lay it out amid the clutty confusion that night an blame it on us. Wouldn be worse than what they do in them big old battles. Like the Trojan War. Where they ballisto dead bodies in over the wall. Or even hog tied live ones screamin through the air to make em shit from fear. Alls fear in love and war.

Sarah Maldon. She get truly spooked after the smashin. Keep addin curtain upon curtain to her windows. Stitch up factory overrun burlap to cover up the lace. An that aint good enough. Next she drape swags a cut baize over the rods without even stitchin it. Bens gone all that time. Channel blockades is good for his private dealins up an down the coast. Aint no French cannon come to help either side. When Im back from Lyington Sarah get someone to wheel me an my things to her house. Says I can stay till I see if Sheppeys old place be vacant from where I can wheel myself to the high road an into town an back without needin any help. But what she mean is until Ben come back. Sarah got a way about her like you got to lift her up to carry her over the mud. What be with them curtains I says when Im sittin in the dark parlor sweatin an lookin round. To keep the night out Corbel she says all trembly quiet an firm. Well they aint no holdin back the night I says. Long swordll slice right through. Slip slop all them curtains be ribbons on the floor. But I keep the windows tight she says. Glass got no answer to a batterin but a shatterin

I says. You seen that at the smashin. She says well I could put up some shutters. I says then you dont need curtains. She says curtains you can peep out but they cant peep in. I says any road Sarah you got so many layers hung no one be lookin out or in nor breathin fresh air neither.

Thats when Sarah an thems livin up behind Stone Hill. Now days theres the new iron works there. Melted iron flow into the little pig iron troughs runnin off the sow ditch. Black blasted ground all round the place. Noise all the time. Shoutin. Iron pigs clankin when theys tossed on the carts. Cart axles squeakin as theys hauled to the line. Seem like most a the sweet places you recall is all dug up or got somethin black dumped on top of em. Shes happier to read me letters from Ben than I am to hear em. Seem hes the only one who make her laugh. I dont even try. That lady get me serious in a serious way. Or sittin on the porch therell be the chaffinch eatin out a her hand. Or inside after the rain the skyll light up again an we open the windows to hear the birds *sweet melody* as Sarah call it. Most folk thats all they know. Colin grab her arm an protest. But mama melody mean sweet he says to her. *Meli* is honey in Greek. Did you know that Mister Penner he ask. Sure an dur I did not know that I says. But it be almost the same in French. I know he says. My papa tell me.

Or we might listen to them prestissimos young Colins

learnt to rouse out a the pianoforte. How Sarah wish Ben be there to hear it. How glad I am he aint. Though Ben got no ear for music she says. But Colin has the slender fingers for it. Dont you Collie dear she says. Show your fingers to Mister Penner. Almost as long as yours she smiles to me. Any time I face that smile I know I aint good enough for her. Watchin Colin fingerin his keys. Dont need no music master now. Poor thing hes got to squint over all his music. But children they dont complain at nothin. Hearin the dazzle. Speed along.

Before the smashin and before Sarah curtain up the place to a hot box William Dogg stop there once. Ben bring Dogg when hes hidin from someone down Big Town. Creditors or editors he says. Both want to slice your flesh and lay it on the scale. But no. Not that. I flee the very devil. He may purr like a puss licking cream but behind his back he dips his tail in pitch to write your numbers down. Trundles ever after me on hob nail boots he says. Tack tack tack tack tack. I hear him coming always as I go. Dogg an Is sittin one late afternoon as the sun drop through the trees an a lacy light sift through the frills an ringlets of Sarahs breezy curtains. Hand made lace. The kind you cant get no more. Though nine from ten cant tell no difference from machine made now. White patterns swivel on the floor an in the window while we sit there in two parlor chairs all afternoon suckin up that sweet black rum Dogg got the jeroboam of propped sideways crosst a treadle arm between the two of us so we can tip it to our lips without spillin any but what you can lick up quick. Little did I know hes about to join the ancient battle twixt light an dark right there in the Maldons parlor. I myself Dogg says. I smuggle shards of Big Town dark in my frayed pockets. Some of it falls through the holes. The rest is ballast for my voyage. He pull some wads a writin paper from his pockets an fling em on the floor an jump up an down stompin em. May they choke upon these pages. May my words fry their bowels until they leak into their shoes he shouts. Big Town he says screwin up his lips an eyes. The noble battlements erected by King Ludd himself so long ago are buried under stinking excrement. Now its nothing but whore mongers. Horse stealers an coney catchers. Cozeners. Nut grabbers. Black mogulers an silly billys of every stripe he says. You can see the flames illuminatin Doggs world in his quiverin face.

> *A staunch and floating iron dream*
> *Yet will sink without a gleam*

I pick that one up from the floor an it chill me. A course Dogg didn know anything about us Iron Boys. But even back then I had a feelin about the fate of iron dreams. An you couldn ask Dogg what he mean by anything. He just shout at you. *Mean* he says an thump his fist. *Mean.* The world sinks. Black meanness of the soul is all we know. We are murdered daily by spiritual accountants and toad lickers.

Them light patterns is a pretty sight movin down the wall an wigglin on the floor an thats all there is to it you might say. But when youre sunk into your chair behind a daylong guzzledown youre lookin out through two glowin knotholes. Dogg start to chant an soon I join him. *Swatch* he says. *Twill an grille.* An I know what hes talkin about. *Weave* I says. *Shimmer. Spill* he says. *Secret ingot. Dapple* I says. *Panel. Lozenge* he says. *Feather. Spangle. Frond* I says an things is gettin fierce. *Quilt* I says an looks him in the eye. *Powder* I says. *Shards an dust.* That aint so good but I cant help myself. Doggs angry now. I can feel the clinch of his teeth in my own jaw. *Granulation. Counterpoint. Filmy embosture* he says. Now hes pointin to em as he names em. Darin me. *Rood screen* I says. *Winnowing. Filigree.* Hes stuck there so I get out three more quick ones. *Branch an coin an golden shred* I says. Dogg swell hisself up an turn beetroot an stop breathin till he look bug eyed dropsical. *Puckered rubber baby bubbles* he rasp out an we rolls on the floor coughin from laughin cause they aint no more light through the curtain any road. What can I say. Down in black rum youre sunk in wet stone thoughts an seein things that others dont.

I says Sarah you got to open up your windows. She says I cant Corbel I dont want to look. What happen to your shutters I says. She says Ben took em off to make a benches for the wagon. Well it pain me sure an dur. Cause them curtains in her eyes now too. You try an talk to her about it she just peel some more potatoes in the dark. Or polish the gleamin table till it grow dull. One time I part the layers an point Sarah out the big bare walnut tree. See that tree its dropped its curtains now I says. Like Im talkin to a child. Oh Corbel Im afraid to look she says. I feel naked like that big wet branch up there she says. Its like a claw is coming here to get at me. You see that old nest stuck in the crook up there she says. Been there five or six years I guess. But now its like a fat black bug an I want to smash it. I just cant stand to look at it. I had a terrible dream she says. Corbel you cant tell anyone. Right up by the sulphur spring there was a grouse nest. But it had seven plover eggs in it. I stand there not knowin what to do she says. The plover must have laid there after the grouse. Im suppose to take the eggs to hatch but I cant look. Bare trees all seem like spindles thats spun all the thread off their spools. All the thread is piling up around me. I cant carry the eggs so theyre going to die unborn.

Corbel you know Colin an Lark they love you she says. But I never told you there was another one. Thats what that nest remind me of. Black botch of it hung up there against the white sky. No birds come to it now. You see why I have to keep the curtains she says. Oh Corbel when they carried you off to Lyington oh oh oh. She move her head up an down sobbin on my shoulder. I rub her back an tell her Ill knock that bad nest down though I dont know how Ill do it with no legs to climb on an in fact I never do.

Come Easter time Milky wheel me up the hill an I can see from the top that all the curtainin is gone. Even the old lace. Just bare windows gleamin inside an out. They was havin a egg party. Children hangin blue twisty paper everwhere an little dollop pots with all the colors you can think of is sittin on benches an boxes an ladder steps an tables. The boys is clappin their wooden swords together wild on account a the masks theys tryin to keep on straight with the other hand. What theys really tryin is to get the girls give em the eggs hidden in their skirts.

> *Give a golden egg*
> *Or the devil scratch your leg*
> *Egg upon a plate*
> *Or the devil burn your gate*

Theys a dove in a spun sugar cage an the winner get to pull the sugar sticks off the side until the bird fly off. Older friend a Colins is jugglin eggs with them old comet wine bottles an thowin em fancy to another lad who thow em back to him in a circle theys makin there in the air. But a egg slip loose an fly off an splat yellow right across the parlor window. So while Im scrubbin off the window with vinegar Im ponderin the skill a jugglin uncooked eggs an wine bottles an that friend a Colins give me a quick wink.

Theres somethin dark hang in the empty square long after Withys is burnt an brung down an the rubble is carted off an stacked up an stolen. It aint like

Rumnilla the Dutch Town witch an her hex. This be more like after a badgers carcass is done rotted away under the house you dont smell it any more but theys still a kind a taste in the shag when youre puffin on your pipe or on the spoon when youre eatin the last a your peas. Like the smell at the butchers of blood runnin down them white troughs next to the slabs.

Nine months tween the time the factorys brought down an when Withy march in his new architects an countin men. Cant say now if that be short time or a long time an not because a the missin clock. But whatever time it was youd a thought the old clear air would a come back over the square where it been baffled an denied so long. But it never do. Dead ground. Withys first factory they build it like I tell you brick by brick up the scaffold. Cartin every part in on flat wagons an stackin em by hand. Back then its mortal man what turns the wrench to bolt the cam shaft to the piston rod an put it into place. Even them bricks was hand pressed in Bell Misty. But the second time they got machines to press the brick. Machines to stir the mortar. Machines to spit it on your trowel. Machines to cut the pipe an spin the bolts. Whole world run by steam pressure now it seem. Maybe I get me some Black Wopper size steamin leg pistons. Why not.

All my years a wanderin I never do go to Child Town till Milky wheel me there one day. Child Town just be one a them turns you dont take if you wasnt born there. You dont need to go an they dont want you. Im wonderin if its about a new name. Without sayin nothin Milkys fixed two big dogs in a harness frame which he attach to my chair an with him pushin behind an me snappin a little whip in the air once in a while we make our way even over the ruttier cross tracks. I wish I could be walkin on my own feet full up beside him like before so I can pat him on the head. Now he could pat me on the head. Dog on the left is bigger so I keep pullin harder on his rein but that just make the littler dog want to stop an scratch hisself.

You take the lane to Peterlawn but you turn off at the broke down tower about a third a the way on the left. Then youre on a wide raggedy path aint never been improved but aint never been abandoned neither. Lads an lasses bustle up an down on all sorts a business. No sign board. They dont call the place Child Town. They dont call it nothin that I know of. Its just where they all be. So we get up to where theys some type a canvas swung like a awnin from tree to tree shelterin the lane under which theres tables. Young miss is writin a letter for a snifflin boy. Older lad is tradin wedges a cheese for buckets a pig berries. Two boys is raisin baskets up by pulleys to a little house in a tree which got a slant roof an windows with flower pots on ledges with ribbons around em. Someones hangin out the window pullin on the rope. Two girls walk up with a tray a sweet oat cakes an offer Milky one. Theys too shy to look at me so I just take a cake an give the near one a pinch on her bum. Young master an mistress is playin a gavotte on a fiddle an a fife an three four girls is dancin. A course I sink back into thoughts a Nancy an me on the bank that afternoon. So long ago. But thinkin a her just aint gonna stop I guess. A naked tot is bangin a spoon on a iron kettle while he sit laughin in a mud puddle which interrupt the rhythm somewhat. All in all Milkys leadin me through a merry scene under a fair sky though he tell me of the older boys on the outskirts whos always makin trouble. Then them dogs start yippin up an bumpin each other an chewin the harnesses. Glad to be back home I guess so Milky untie em an let em loose. I aint seen Milky since the smashing so I cant help myself. Is there or aint there a Gunny I ast. He dont say nothin for a time. Just wheel me down the track into more dispersed territory. Do you or dont you got a sister I says. You can make out huts an tents an some shacks off the path a ways. Looks like theys runnin this part right well. What happen on the roof with those men an the tar I says. Is you the one use to sleep on a shelf at the Lion. Aint you tired a pushin me. Im gettin angry at him cause ever since the smashin I aint had no answers to nothin.

He turn my wheels so Ise in a patch a sun but my eyes is shaded by the leafage. Then he climb up on a fat low branch aint much above my head an lie down on it. Do you got a mother Mister Penner he ask. No I dont I says. I mean I do like we all do but I never knowd who she is I says. What do you know about it he says to me. What is it youre askin me I says to him. Tell me a story of it he says. Just lookin at him lyin there with his chin on his hands make me think back to bark boats an crab apples so I start talkin. Some a what I say is real an some a driftin dream an I aint sure I know the difference no more.

I got drug off to the sea shore once I says to him. When they try to give me away. They told me Id like the sea shore but I didn like it one jit. Wernt a bush to tie a ribbon to I says. End a the world it look like I says. Smell like it too. Flappy stinkin stuff lyin where it drift in to rot. Doin no body no good. Big slick blubbery thing turned inside out over a rock except for the two hairy eyes still starin at me as it quiver an flop. Even at that age I knew he wouldn never get back in the sea an wernt meant for land. I wouldn stop cryin for a long long time they tell me. Nobody want me cause I wont stop cryin. Then Im sittin on a bluff next to a man I dont know with his big hands on my little shoulders. The breeze dont stink so much up there. When the sun start to drop I start a shiverin. Just sittin there watchin the waves come. Such a vast thing as the sea I never seed before an somehow I feel better bein small an watchin it. Dont know what Im doin with this man. Gray white birds is skreakin sad an sharp an that high cry dont seem to come from inside em. Just part a the whole sorrow. I want to cry but my throats too tight. Ever time I hear the squeakin machines I think a them sorrowful sea birds. Way them waves crash over an over. Over an over. Seem all wrong to me. Into the land then slidin back out. Seem all backwards. Theys somethin not showin thatll never show. Somethin twisted up inside em. To see em right you got to see em flow an bubble quiet up through the little pebbles then jump in the air with a foamy shush an leap backwards an curl down into a uncrashin wave that slide into itself an roll with a swell out to the far horizon. Thats what we should see. We see it all backwards. Sun go down an Im afraid a the whole world. It seem so close by an so far. I dont want it to be close or far. I want it to go away. The man leave sayin only wait here lad. He gots thick rough trousers of a odd color. Rip in the knee. Wet about the ankles. Thats all I remember.

That aint about your mother Milky says. I do forget what Im spose to be tellin him but I says to him yes it is. An he says why. I says it be about her because a the man sittin next to me whos sellin me because my mother she dont know how to give me away I says. I says it be about her because a the waves goin backwards. I go backwards too Milky says. Backwards is forwards I says just to make sure he dont misunderstand. He says to me you dont mind if someone else push you for a while do you Mister Penner. Just so they dont push me backwards I says.

So he calls a fellow over. Biggern Milky though he may not be older. I dont get to see much since hes behind me an dont say nothin. He lean me back so he can bump me over the ruts an hummocks cause we be off on one wild ride. Milky keep stalkin ahead like a bold scout an then turnin back with a little boy smile so I close my eyes an try to abide the shakin. Alls I see is sun an leaf shadow flitter over my lids. Kind a thing would put you to sleep if you wernt bumpin.

Next time the fellow tilt me down I ope my eyes an there two wrapped up ladies is sittin on a stone bench next to a fountain that gots your unswaddled grinnin fat cupid babies pourin water from a pitcher. Its Silvy an the Widow. I wont believe it at first cause I been bumpin along with my eyes tight an might be seein sun blotches. But there they sit a talkin to each other like always. First thing I want to do is pull my blanket up over my head to hide my face which has seen so much since I last seed them two but aint seen much of a mirror. However a blanket be just so long an not longer on account a the clickin a the ratchets which stop it for the cuttin blade an start another one. If I pull it over my head itll show I got nothin but a lack a legs down there. I guess my face is better than my legs but I like to hide everthing before Silvy turn around an see whats left a me. How long has it been. May be Silvy now she gots a fellow who give her what I didn. Though some how it dont seem so. Even if you stitch the time up in numbers. Is them numbers big or small. It be like that comet which move fast an slow or the factory which move fast an slow or like the waves which move fast an slow an forwards an backwards an dissolve everthing an wash it out to sea. Then Milky he say somethin I dont think I hear but it shake my frame like that factory wall come down on me. Thats my mama Milky says pointin to my sweet Silvy. Yesterday she come an say she is. Would she lie to me Mister Penner he ask. I cant say nothin back. But Im thinkin only the simple hearted truth ever come out a her. Yet that be several once upon a times ago. Things is changed. May be she can lie now like the rest of us. May be she only didn lie to me because she left.

How old be you Milky I says to him. I dont know Mister Penner he says. Could be my mama she can tell me. I reckon she know my name. If she be my mama. Do you think shes pretty he asts me. Milky I says to him. I know who them ladies be. An I know I tell you Id help get you a new name. I wernt lyin I says to him. An that lady she wouldn lie about bein your mama. Only kind a lie you or she or Id telld be a lie to protect your truth. What you carry around inside a you that no one else know an if they did they mightn be so gentle with it. Might stamp it in the dirt an kick at it for fun. I aint lookin at him an he aint lookin at me. We boths just lookin at Silvy an the Widow. An theys lookin at each other. That table over there under the tree I says to him. Im pointin at what aint a proper table but one a them big spools they wind that new twisted iron cable on. You wheel me over there I says. Then go an get that lady whos your mama an the other lady an bring em here. Did you tell em bout me I ask him but hes scampered off.

Cant say my thoughts is madly workin. I dont even want to watch. Just me in the shade an remembrin the ladder up to a sack stuffed full a meadow bells. Silvy shes gonna say it be that Iron Seed I keep when she tell me to get rid of it. Thats why I lose my legs. There be some truth to that. Iron Seed. What she see in my eyes that night. Not good not good not good she say. But I be already magnetized for times to come. May be thats why she leave. An I know you wont believe it. But its only when I ope my eyes an she be there before me with Milky an the Widow by her side that I know the truth of it. An I says to Milky you know what. An he says no what. An I says again to him you know what. Cause I still cant look at Silvy. Standin there she an the Widow is bright shadows in the light. An grinnin he says no what. An I says you got a name already. An I dont want to hear no more about it.

When I ast Silvy where she an her mother been all them long years till yesterday she put her finger to my lips. Oh dear Corbel I dont like to say it to you she says. Still got her French music but a flatter sound on some a the words. I hope you do forgive she says. An what do you say to that but a squeeze an a kiss cause I dont like to talk to her a my own doins an undoins neither. One thingd lead to another an then I be tellin her about Bovie an the puppy dog an the age a iron an that I will not do. Man become machinery but done is done. May be we start our own age a gold.

It wernt long before Corbel an Silvy Penner an Milky Penner an Widow Dedoray wes all livin in the tall dark house left empty by Rose Stonewarden when she move off to Runny Pumps with her sister Mildred whos the last one I talk to about the speech a birds I guess with her Mister Penner do birds kiss kind a mess. An her baby the one with long gray hair like a old man. Just imagine six hunnerd an sixty six crows sittin in six bare trees watchin you. Numbers an birds. When crows scatter it be like them five minute marks grown fat an restless get flung off the devils clock.

At my ripe age Stone Mallows is the first house I ever live in. Or the downstairs part of it any road. We all find our places in it. Stone Mallows we call it after Rose Stonewarden an her good dish a bog mallows with stewed carrots an onions an port. Silvy an me we aint actually man an wife cause a some papers she an I would have to get that we aint got. No matter. Veuve present me with a dowry chest full a true gold red China silk an finest point de venise lace. Privately Im thinkin what do I do but put a bib on a beagle. But I keep it to myself. Widow she say she never in her life have a proper lock. Times indeed is new so we get the lock smith to conjure up a German job he make three fancy keys for. Milky say he want one too but I says to him son you dont need a key. I seen you on Withys roof an slidin down that firework rope you still aint explain to me. I rub his head an I says to him if there aint nobody here an the door be locked you just climb the tree an come in through that upstairs window. I seen you do that any ways I says. But what about them men on the roof an the other cauldron a tar. Did anybody get splashed with it I ast him. No papa he says to me. We keep em busy dodgin apples.

So Im sittin in my house. Puffin on a pipe which I never did regular before. Kegs a frothy brown beer down cellar. Time to think about it all. It be like the very dream I get from Withys turnip clock. House at the end a my long road. Now I got a real key. First place I feel I might stretch my legs full out I aint got em. Milky nail up a ramp to the porch my wheels fit on just fine. But restin there one afternoon or other as the sun mingle down amongst the mud an wet trees on Pollard Street I cant stop thinkin a my old friend Teddy. Eddard Weedy. Sad about him. Sad about a lot a folk. A letter arrive to me writ by a nurse way down in Brinehaven. Before the smashin. I hadn seed him for six month or so an this letter take three month to find me cause I aint got no what you call address back then to send it to. It would a had to say like Corbel Penner care a Boot Heel Lay By. Eddard in his first distress he tell the nurse his mamas name an town an forget that she dont know me. He never take me to meet her. But I make out in that short page Teddy aint got long to live an when I get down to Brinehaven hes dead in the ground. Paupers field though later it come out there be a soldiers pension somewhere. Nurse tell me Eddards numbers three thirty four an she show me the way holdin up her stiff white skirts through the mud. Nothin but numbers on the stones there. I guess you got to pay to get a name I says to her. I must a get misted an mashed a bit cause I was kickin at the damn stone an stompin the dirt up against it an then she put her hand on my arm an squeeze it hard. She wernt kind but she were there. I says well Eddard he get hisself a biggish number any road. She says its big now but there be a lot more on the way. Its Eddard who point me out that the mornin star be the same as the evenin star just gone round on itself much like the moon in its circles. Dont seem like that could be. That star change so much one time to the next. Up an down an bright an dim an green an yellow. Look differnt ever time. Just like the moon got differnt oracles in its differnt lights an sizes. Some times pullin you an some times not. Never twice the same an thats the truth. An yet it do come round the same. Time after time. Good thing to remember Teddy by. Fierce astronomer.

Sittin on my porch in the mornin light them first days at Stone Mallows I watch that brick wall a Withys new South Plant he call it rise up in the only sky I can see down Pollard Street between the roof edge a the old warehouse an the sign board a the Pump an Piston. I know I be seein less an less a that patch a sky as time go on an thisll be the way a the world until we some how brick over the sky itself. Pipe our smoke out to the stars. Its clear they wont be no more mornin star down Pollard Street. Them brick rows rise back an forth like some kind a slow shuttle. On some fine evenins that brick wall pattern shine in the light like perfect silkeen cloth. Gots to be some beauty in the works. Days pile up on numbered days with no remainder. No one look back no more to think on what did happen. Time was the Iron Boy tale be the most important thing I got. Now the Iron Boy bands dissolved. All this make me tired to think upon. Truth is I dont much care no more. We done done what we done done. An you be the only one I ever tell it to. Machines they spin servitude into fine lace made out a big numbers an it go one way only. Never do you get steam back from the shuttles. An you get no coal by burnin cloth. New world be made out a new brick carried by mechanical hodsmen twelve feet tall. Even the same old people you once know be new when they dont recall nothin or pretend not to. What can you call New Billy now. New New Billy be head a the waste cloth at South Plant. Manufactory aint even *Withy & Co* no more. He get himself sucked up an puffed out by his own vision. Off to France half the time. New names *Global Pilfer*. That branch a his family must a had some weight. More than Meadows or Cogent any road. Fancy new sign but they dont put up another clock. Withy had enough a that I wager. There is a steam horn for the shifts though.

Them dang birds. They dont talk no more but they do show me one more thing. Dumb doves try to nest on a ledge above the porch corner. That nest get blowed or washed out ever time theres wind or rain but them doves just come right back next day an build again. Five times I seed it an the nest come down each time. Finally them eggs get smashed an you know how hard dried egg is to get off your porch. But them smashed up eggs remind me a Easter at Maldons an the rhymes a that jugglin fellow.

> *Intery mintery cuttery corn*
> *Apple seed an iron thorn*
> *Tick tock limber lock*
> *Five fat birds in a flock*
> *Sit an sing by a spring*
> *O U T and in again*

So somethin in my blood tell me we got to stage an attack on *Global Pilfer*. But nothin big. Not with hammer pike an gun. We seen that the best destruction we gotll only make em build it bigger an stronger. Fact is they now put guard chambers round about both buildins. An the machine rooms is divided up more now. They say that be for supportin walls so the factory wont fall so readily upon itself. But you know also it be to keep folk separated at their labors. Cut off from the sight a one another. Supportin walls an separation. Aint it wry how purposes align like that. So I send the family out. Each on a mission. Silvy to find four common churl eggs. Four because her blue dress it got these four lace edge I dont know what you call ems. Scallops slung across the upper part. An the way its stitched there she got four little pockets that four churl eggsll fit right into. Milky I tell him get me three explodin eggs. Not knowin what he may arrive with but knowin I dont want to know. An Widow Dedoray well you can guess. A golden egg. Or didn I tell you Dedoray it mean to lose your gold or some such thing. Me I roll my rump down the ramp one morn an make my way to the Pump an Piston. Who do I see but Desmond Carke sittin at a table with Timothy Twist as if their tracks has long been in the same direction. I raise a finger to Desmond so Twist dont see. I want to get out a there clean but when I try to buy boiled eggs from the big jar thats always on the shelf with beetroot an onion the man push back my coin. With a nod he let me know theys bein bought by yon table. I wheel myself around an theres Twist starin through me like he always do. But now I know I aint wrong to discern the barest tickle of a smile twitchin the edge a his lip. Carkes smilin also. So I gots my two eggs.

Next clear night when the moons sliced sharp in half like a potato pie we slink out to four quarters a the new manufactory. Not South Plant but the main buildin. Aint so simple now as once be. Got differnt angles an connectin halls an guard turrets an blind buttresses. But the important part is the cardinal directions an the new factory still hew to em as the old roads make clear. At the final stroke a ten we do our deed. Not midnight like it should be cause we got to get Veuve to her sleep an Silvy try to bend our Milky to a more proper way a life. Though with scant success may I say. Each alone in the night we dont look dangerous. An who will say if we is or if we aint. Silvy fling her churl eggs one by one to smash on the brickwork a the northern side. You see them splotches to this day. I do think they will stand the test a time. Three bright powder flashes bang up from the western reach an echo back from the distances. Then three colored streamers whistle through the air up by the moon. Shootin sparks in differnt colors an them smokin eggs whirl round in circles. If smashin times come back again an Milky join another band his skills will shine. Me I hire a Child Town lad to wheel me to the east entrance. Tell the guard who come out I give him two red eggs for a twist a bright shag. Good trade at that hour of a nice quiet night. Rollin back home I puff my pipe. Yolk inside them eggs is now inside the belly of a man who be inside the factory lookin out through sleepy eyes.

What Veuve do is she have a smith melt down a pound a bangles an gild an egg fit right in your hand.

With her thin widow arms she lob it underhand through the big window in the southern wall. I didn hear the crash that night but saw the jagged hole next day. We get back home our separate ways an Widow pour some old champagne. Even Milky get a taste. Through the open windows a Stone Mallows that night floatin above the clankin factory noise there come sweet unnumbered breezes an sweet sleep for all. Our tale be over sure an dur.

> *My anvil an hammer lie declined*
> *My bellows has quite lost its wind*
> *My fires extinct an forge decayed*
> *My vice be in the dust all laid*
> *My coals is spent my iron gone*
> *My nails be drove my work be done*

I aint that quiet yet but I do try an keep in mind how things look just before the roof give way an the world fall on me. I didn know it then but now I see it clear. One star through the gap in the beams gleamin down. Just one. Right there. I wonder what its name be. Teddy would a known.

Differnt devils differnt times. Sign boards change. Green Lions now Red Rooster. The big walnut tree with Black Woppers eyes get cracked by lightnin then sawed up. Now its nothin but a weed choked stump crawlin with ants. New trees along Withy Lane grow wide an thow dapple shade over the carts rumblin in an out all day. Old Barley Moats is dead. Cecily took off with a waterman. Millers son is tappin the kegs at the Rooster. Come a time an that time soon even you wont care no more. Then we can sing a real song.

Silvy an me we get our blood pumpin once an again. Her on top a me a course. No more ladders to heaven. But Im happy at Stone Mallows. Silvy she teach French to folk who seem to want it now. So called business men. I do love to hear her talkin silver French riddles with them folk. It mean more not knowin what shes sayin. Veuve she seem happier than before. Get all sorts come by our place Sunday afternoons. Music an rhyme an scientific talk. French folk too. Mostly Im happy to sit on the porch an welcome em. Timothy Twist come once for cakes an sherry. Gets everone to laugh but dont say much you can remember. Please the ladies though. Even Withy have a invitation though he aint show up yet. Id like to see New New Billy. They say hes always at the factory now. Wonder what happen to his Trojan Horsy. New world now for everone. You dont go forward cept through going back. Waves at the sea shore teach me that. An tryin to tell you this tale.

Milky hes my boy. He be my real Iron Seed. Hes a rankle wonder. Only good reason to grow old is to watch him grow. An what do you grow but up. *For my days is consumed like smoke. My heart is smitten an withered like grass so I forget to eat my bread.* You might say that. *Im like a pelican in the wilderness. Im like a owl in the desert.* You might say that. *I hop like a sparrow alone on the house top.* I wouldn say that. But *Ive eaten ashes like bread an bread like ashes an mingled my drink with my weepin* an who cant say that.

But still. It be bettern what they say itll be. Cause they always give you the dark outside but inside you gots the light. An if them birds ever try to tell me differnt Ill tell em *Ricky did it. Ricky did it. Ricky did it.* An cause a bein contrary little peckers theyll say back *Whos Ricky. Whadideedo. Whos Ricky. Whadideedo.* This time theyll have to figure it out for themselves.

ACKNOWLEDGEMENTS

The madcap invention of print can't possibly convey proper thanks to the following: Flora Strong Farmer, for jokes; Willard Blair Frick, for words; Lois McClure White, for stories and birds; Ian, Leslie, Kayla, Kristi, and Andy Frick, and Leon White, for long-term belief and support; Martin Pick, and the Charles Pick Fellowship at the University of East Anglia, England, during which much of the first draft was written; Barry, for a perceptive question that prompted a major turn of plot; William Gass and the other master artists and associates of Residency 111 at the Atlantic Center for the Arts, for invigorating encouragement; Sven Birkerts, my longtime palinuric pal; Amy Friedman, for powerful leonine protections; Sarah Gaddis, for reading the very first paragraphs in ivy-choked Castle Cochran; Jessica McIntyre, for reminders that cliffs of fall can indeed be fathomed and even cheerfully soared over; Allan Jalon, for a spontaneous theatrical viewpoint; the brilliant Clare Foster, for the most incisive critique this writer has ever received; Pam Scott, for tuning the sheaths; Quendrith "Papercuts" Johnson, for a continent's worth of something I can't quite put a name to; Captain "Wm. Bligh" Danielsen, for many years of stimulating circumferentiality; Diane Botnick, for mind-meld and succinct enthusiasm; my LACMA Publications colleagues, for personal and professional encouragement; Kirkpatrick Sale, for *Rebels Against the Future* (Addison-Wesley, 1995); Humphrey Jennings, for the uniquely illuminating *Pandaemonium* (Free Press, 1985); Lynn Larsen, for helpful last-minute suggestions; and last, first, and in between, Melody Sumner Carnahan and Michael Sumner, for their friendship and the cheerful feeding of soup to nuts, as the best publishers have always done.

—Thomas Frick, Los Angeles, 2011

other books in the QUADRANTS SERIES

Quicksand
Robert Ashley

Only a Messenger
Sumner Carnahan

If Nothing Changes
L. K. Larsen

Q+1
short works from the
Quadrants Series authors

alere flammam

"I think POCKET BOOKS are perfectly excellent. Their format, type, etc., are admirable, and I feel sure they are doing a grand job in giving everybody in the country a chance to get a library together."

—Jan Struther, author of *Mrs. Miniver,* April 1943

"You never realized how much you can trust a BOOK—it has no wires or transistors or digital screen—it never breaks down, you don't have to pay a monthly fee to read it, no on/off switch, it's your friend in fact."

—Mark Weber, author of *Plain Old Boogie Long Division,* February 2011